Bury Me in Montauk

Jay Dowski

Chapter 1: Bury Me in Montauk

Friday night was the last time I ever saw my father. He was unable to communicate with spoken words, but his eyes were open and aware. As I spoke, he looked at me with understanding. An occasional wince and wrinkle of the brow served as responses to my words. It didn't matter much that this was all he could do. Honestly, I felt as if the words that I was speaking were inadequate themselves. I felt as if I was just reciting the same lines you'd hear in a movie. You know, the movie where the thirty-seven-year-old son goes to see his distant father in the hospital for one last time knowing that he was going to die soon, the air in the room being an open battleground for anger, guilt and resentment. All makes for an awkward moment. I had one eye on the clock.

Mom has been dead for two years now. Even though Brookhaven, New York is about a two hour drive to Elizabeth, New Jersey, we might as well have been on each side of the country. I hadn't seen my father for the last twenty-four months of his life and the truth is that the non-visits didn't differ much from the times that we did see each other; it was the same amount of 'quality time' spent. My mother tried to get me to come see him more before she died and when she was about to pass, she made me promise I'd take care of him after her death. The truth is, the man wouldn't let me get close to him. Or maybe I just didn't try hard enough.

After mom passed, I spent the next year and two months worried about being laid-off from my job as a customer service agent at a travel agency. I collected hours upon hours of overtime work; every day when I finally did get home, I only had enough energy left to pour three fingers of Jameson into a glass of ice and watch pre-recorded T.V. shows. However, all of my worrying and hard work was useless because I ended up getting laid-off anyway. That was ten months ago and the last thing I wanted to do since then was be in my father's presence and have to answer his questions about my current life situation or any events of my life for that matter. It wasn't the questions that I was afraid of, I sure as hell know they would be brief, insensitive and to the point. No, it was the judgmental sigh that was sure to follow my answers. Even when he got sick I always made an excuse to myself about why I couldn't come see him.

My brother did the same. If anyone was better than me at treating a visit to dad's like a visit to the proctologist, it was my brother, Joe.

But, I finally made it. I was a few years late, but a few hours just in time. Like I said, he was alive and his eyes were open as I asked him how he was feeling (what a dumb question) and whether I could get him anything (as if it would save his life). We did, however, have one brief, honest moment right before I left the hospital. I told him that I had to leave because I had to drive back to Long Island to get home and go to work in the morning. I admitted to him that I was laid-off at the travel agency and for the past ten months I've been working as a flower delivery man for a local florist in Brookhaven. I declared to him, 'I know that it's nothing to be proud about, but then again I never really did anything in my life that was of much significance and nobody knows that more than you.' He didn't wince or wrinkle his brow after that one, come to think about it he didn't even blink he just sort of stared straight ahead, motionless, as if deep in thought. Maybe I decided to be so honest with him at that moment because I knew that he *couldn't* respond. Shortly thereafter, I managed to place my hand on his shoulder, say goodbye without eye contact, and drive out of Jersey like it was a leper colony. I thought about giving him a kiss on the forehead or something, I really did, but I didn't know how.

The call came two days later on Sunday night just as I was closing my eyes to try and get a few hours of sleep. The hospital nurse was professional and sweet as she delivered the news and after I hung up, sleep eluded me. I laid in my bed alone, no companion. All I had was my thoughts, and they were not kind to me. What did I think of in those hours? Anything and everything at the same time which, when done right, feels like a blizzard of mental white noise.

This Monday morning, right now, I'm walking into the flower shop. It's 9:00 a.m. and the only thing I can think about is gathering my first batch of deliveries, loading up my car and heading straight to the local 7-11 to get my treasured first cup of coffee. The first sip of the first cup of coffee is pretty much the first thing I think about every day when I wake up and today that first cup is going to be extremely tall and that first sip is going to be incredibly long.

For my first run, I have four deliveries total. I quickly write down the addresses of all of them. There are three bouquets going to Brookhaven and one going to Holtsville. I get the first three Brookhaven deliveries done in thirty minutes. The coffee begins to expand the blood vessels of my brain on the way to Holtsville. As I pull up to the destination, I see it's an office building. I leave my Toyota Avalon idling in the circle up front, enter through the main entrance and approach the security desk.

"I have a flower delivery for a Mr. Harold Gordon, going to the office of Island-wide Medical Group."

The security guard checks the book in front of him.

"That's office number 350. Take these elevators right behind you up to the third floor and when you get to the top you're going to make a left and head down the long hallway, the office should be on your right hand side."

I thank him and hop into the elevator. When the doors open to the third floor, I head left. Number 331 is on the left... 332 is on the right... I walk along... 335... 336... The distance in between the office doors becomes more and more spread out and for a moment I wonder whether I'm currently getting set up to be whacked. I have a fantastical vision that when I get to office number 350 and open the door the entire room is going to be covered in plastic wrap and two men in white biohazard suits and pistols will be standing there to 'welcome' me.

341... 342... 343...344... I pass by a big pane of clear glass on my right hand side that allows me to look out onto the back parking lot and clearly see the back entrance to the office building... 347...348... The door to 350 has no name on it, just the number. I open it up... no plastic, no biohazard suits, just a receptionist's desk and a small waiting area. The receptionist is a forty-something-year-old nurse with curly hair. She stops chewing her gum and smiles when I approach.

"Good morning, how may I help you?" she asks.

"Good morning, I have a flower delivery for… Harold Gordon."

Her eyebrows squeeze together and erase the spot of flesh in between each other. Usually the receptionist just smiles and says, 'ohhh, okay,' and then suddenly becomes giddy at the idea of being the lucky person to deliver the news to their co-worker that somebody has sent them flowers, but not this time. I could tell that she had never heard of Harold Gordon.

"Harold who?"

At this moment, a doctor enters into view from the back hall carrying a handful of folders. He walks behind the receptionist and rummages through the files of a bookcase; slipping the folders into files where he sees fit.

I double-check the tag on the flower delivery. "The tag says, Harold Gordon." I triple-check, yep, Harold Gordon.

"I don't know of anybody with that name that works here but let me ask the doctor just to make sure." She begins to get up out of her chair when the doctor turns his head.

"What was the name?" his voice crescendos in surprise.

The receptionist remains seated. "Harold Gordon?" she shrugs her shoulders.

The doctor looks at me... Five seconds go by.

"May I see the name tag?"

"Sure." I take a step closer and place the bouquet of flowers on the desk. He places the folders down in front of him, reaches into his pocket and pulls out his glasses. "Where did you get these?"

"What do you mean?" now I'm confused.

"Where did you get these flowers?"

"I work for a florist. Somebody ordered them and asked us to deliver them to this office. To Harold Gordon."

In this day-and-age I never thought I'd have to explain to another human being the whole 'delivery service' thing and how it worked... especially a so-called 'intellectual' like a doctor.

Squinting behind his glasses that rest upon the bridge of his nose, he examines me as if I was half-naked sitting upon his tissue-papered table. Even the giant mole on his cheek is judging me.

"One moment, please." He turns and disappears into the back.

I look at the receptionist, "Maybe he will find out who they're for."

She shrugs, "Maybe." Then she looks down and returns to her computer.

I scan the waiting room area: a T.V. up in the corner of the ceiling, six chairs lined against the wall, a table full of magazines in the middle. Waiting rooms always sort of creep me out, especially the magazines. Dozens of sick people touching them each day; I could never stomach it enough to ever pick one up. As a patient, whenever I had to go in to see a doctor, I made sure that when I was in the waiting room I kept my hands in my pockets and the only thing that I touched was my ass on the seat- that was it.

Though now that I'm here, I wonder if I should ask the doctor if he would be willing to take a look inside my mouth. I keep feeling this 'thing' at the back of my throat every time I swallow. It feels like a bump of some sorts. I'm constantly looking into a mirror with my mouth wide open trying to see it for myself, but I always come up with nothing... Maybe I'll ask him about it...

A minute of silence passes before the main door of the office opens and the security guard from the front desk steps in. He looks around left to right and when his eyes find me they rest there. He nods.

How's it going?" he asks.

"Good," I hope.

He nods his head up and down in a slow, wave-like motion as he makes his way closer to me.

"It occurred to me that I never asked you to display a valid form of identification when you were downstairs." He holds his hand out to receive.

"Is that customary?" I ask.

"Yes, it is."

The notion doesn't seem ludicrous to me because I've been to a handful of office buildings where I was required to show I.D. So I reach into my pocket and produce my wallet, handing my driver's license over to him.

From behind the receptionist's desk, the doctor returns. He and the security guard make eye contact then the doctor turns his attention to me.

"I need to look at these flowers again," he states.

I walk over and ask him, 'Any luck?' but I already know that he's going to say no. A feeling inside me begins to constrict my blood vessels. The doctor grasps the tag on the flowers within his fingertips and focuses through his eyeglasses.

"What florist did you say you were from?" he answers his question simply by reading the tag, "Towers Flowers."

"Did you find Mr. Gordon?" I ask.

"No, Mr. Gordon is not here. But you can leave the flowers with me."

"I'm sorry, but we don't leave flowers unless the recipient is present. It keeps us out of trouble in case the sender calls and asks about them. We always want to be able to tell the sender that we personally delivered the flowers to the proper person."

That was the truth. I don't feel like being responsible for the flowers in case anything happened to them. Plus, I don't trust the doctor, nor this current situation anymore. It's time to start walking toward the door.

"Thank you, though, have a great day," I force a smile and make a beeline straight for the door, turn the knob and create a space just big enough for me to slip through and close the door behind me. Flowers in hand, I hasten my pace as I walk down the hall and away from the office... Number 350... 348... 347... I hear the door open up behind me and I glance back over my shoulder to see the security guard peak his head out... 346... 345... 344... My attention is turned to the big window pane to my left hand side that overlooks the back parking lot and back entrance to the office building. I notice two black Crown Victorias with red lights flashing on their dashboards. They come to a screeching halt right outside the back entrance of the building. Their doors open and four men run out, two-a-piece, dressed in black suits with black ties. My instincts tell me to look back over my shoulder; the security guard is now running down the hall. My instincts tell me to do the same!

I pump my hands as my feet violently stomp toward the elevators. Screw that, I pass them and barrel through the stairwell door. I don't run down the stairs; I practically jump down them, about seven at a time for three flights. Flower petals spray as the bouquet I'm holding gets tossed about. I don't care about the condition they're in anymore, but for some reason I don't drop them. As I open the door to the ground level, I envision the men in black suits to be standing there ready to tase me, clobber me with Billy clubs or worse, shoot me. But they're not, only a few employees walk across the lobby floor as I do my best Usain Bolt impersonation. My heart races. I don't know what I'm running from, but I know that whatever the case is, running is imperative. As I'm running there's a voice inside my head saying, *Wow, I didn't know you could move like this anymore.* Apparently, I still have my speed as well as my untimely sense of humor.

I approach the glass door that leads outside and pray that it doesn't shatter as I push through it and taste the fresh air. My car, still idling in the circle, waits for me. I open the door, throw the flowers onto the passenger seat, put the car in drive and peel out.

I've never driven like this before. I mean, I've been late to certain events, I've had to go to the bathroom pretty badly and I've ran the occasional red light because of all these things, but right now there's not one rule of the road that applies to me. However, amidst all of this nervous energy I am aware that I need to perform a delicate balancing act. I need to drive like a bat out of hell but I also need to not get caught. I watch out for cops as I blow stop signs, burn rubber and motor well over the speed limit. My mission is to get back to the shop as soon as possible and figure all of this out. I know I haven't done anything illegal, but something or someone has caused a group of people to chase after me.

Or...

The mental lightbulb goes on.

Something has caused a group of people to chase after these flowers.

My thinking shifts back and forth in my mind; the doctor knows what florist I work at and he will surely tell the men in black suits so, I shouldn't go back to the shop. Then again, I haven't done anything wrong and maybe this will all be solved and figured out if I go back and explain to my boss what happened. But it's really not the flowers they're after, right? It is the name: Harold Gordon. Who is he? Who is after him? Who sent these flowers to Harold Gordon and what the hell did Harold Gordon do that it produced such a reaction?

I turn off the main road, onto a side street and pull over. My head turns slightly as my eyes rest upon the now disheveled bouquet of flowers. My curiosity convinces me that the only logical thing I should do next is check the card that's pinned to the front of the bundle of freshly cut stems. Placing the flowers in my lap, I unpin the card and open it up.

It reads:

"If you're reading this then you've currently witnessed the beginning of a series of events that you must see through to the end. There's no forgetting about this, no sweeping it under the rug, and no ignoring it. You cannot stop until you find out the truth and experience it for yourself. Then, I hope, you will take the most significant action. Then, I hope you will do the one thing I couldn't do.

Be careful, be smart, and trust your judgment when dealing with difficult decisions. Do not quit.

Your next destination is 3245 24th Street, Astoria, Queens. When you arrive, together, take the urn and bury me in Montauk..."

Chapter 2: Party of Two

I suspect that the card is from dad. Everything else is a complete mystery to me; Harold Gordon, the men in the black suits, even the address in Astoria is unfamiliar to me. However, I have an idea about who lives there. I put the car in drive and find my way back onto the main road with haste.

I can't go back to the flower shop, I'm sure that is where the men in black suits are headed right now. I'm completely lost, completely puzzled. My brain is racing three times as fast as the speed at which my car is going. I need to take a deep breath and proceed one step at a time. I need to look at it objectively; Harold Gordon is a person of interest. My father knew Harold Gordon and he also knew the mention of his name would get the attention of others. If I can go home I can then settle mysel- oh shit!... I can't go home. I gave the security guard at the doctor's office my driver's license but I never took it back. They know where I work and live.

Well, maybe I can just talk to them. Maybe that's all they want. Maybe all it will take is a five minute conversation of me telling them that I have no idea what is going on and all of this will be over and I can go back to work.

But what if they want to kill me?

Maybe this is all a misunderstanding and they just want to question me.

But what if they want to kill me?

It's probably just a case of mistaken identity.

But what if they want to kill that person?

Well... I didn't really want to work today anyways.

As I continue this internal merry-go-round my external conflicts elevate to another level. In my rearview mirror I see a black Crown Victoria change lanes and get in right behind me. The car inches closer and closer to my tailgate. *They wouldn't bump me, that doesn't happen in real life...* but right on cue, the damn Crown Vic jumps rubber and pushes my bumper! My steering wheel jolts side to side. I regain control and press the gas pedal to the floor to try and create space. They don't speed up to bump me again but they maintain a speed that is now at a distance of about two car lengths behind. In the rearview mirror I can vaguely make out the driver as a clean-shaven man wearing dark sunglasses. In the passenger seat is his partner, shaven as well, but a huskier face. In the midst of trying to get a good look at the men in the car behind me, I neglect the red light at the approaching intersection in front of me. *Slam on the brakes!* I'm about a car length over the white line, the driver of an intersecting car doesn't approve of my driving and blares the horn as they pass by the front of my bumper. The driver throws their hands up and rubber-necks the hell out of me. If they only knew my plight.

Deep breath. I peel my death grip off the steering wheel and look in the rearview again. The black Crown Vic is empty! I swing my head around and just as I make a ninety-degree turn with my neck the butt end of a gun comes crashing through my driver side window and shatters glass all over my lap. The arm holding the gun misses no opportunity to follow through and allow the nose of the gun to find a secure resting place against my cheek. *Holy Shit.*

Regarding any past questions such as, '*What if they want to kill me?*' My answer right now would be, '*I don't think they're afraid to.*'

"Slowly put both of your hands on the steering wheel." His voice is foreign to me. Deep, foreign and frightening. I comply and resume my hard grip on the steering wheel, my vision looks beyond my finger tips and I see a gap in the flow of opposing traffic at the intersection. The light is still red but if ever there was a time to try and escape this current situation, now was it. I move my vision over to the left to see a black blur out of the corner of my eye, it is cold and digs further into my cheek. The other man tries to open the passenger door but it's locked, the man holding the gun to my face slips his other hand into the car and unlocks all the doors with one flick. As soon as the passenger door opens up, I slam on the gas and one second later the gun goes off, firing a hole through my windshield and deafening my left ear! I look both ways and see an intersecting car heading straight for the driver side, quickly, I pull the wheel right and look in the rearview to catch the two men in suits running back to their car. I make sure not to let the gas pedal rise from the floor. Another quick right takes me down a side street. I pray nobody jumps out into the middle of the road because I'm not stopping. About forty yards behind me I see the Black Crown Vic turn down the road in pursuit. My keen driving skills are a result of laser focus; a sudden right and I double pump on the wheel to avoid an old couple crossing the road, a violent left and I escape T-boning a school bus. Ahead I can see a great opportunity: railroad tracks with the lights flashing, the long safety arms are beginning to come down. *I have to make this.* My car and my mind are connected and running at one level: *Go.* Twenty yards away… the arms are half way down and I'm trying to push the gas pedal through the floor of the car. Ten yards… I can't stop now I can only hope that once the front of my car crashes into the arms that they don't stop me cold in my tracks and slingshot me backwards… They don't. I bust through the arms like a four-by-four cracking over Andre the Giant's back. The train itself is about twenty yards away and never T-bones me but rather sets a perfect pick between me and my pursuers long enough to make several turns down several small roads and find a big parking lot. There, I tuck my car away. I can't risk driving it around anymore, they'll be looking for it. Though I imagine that once somebody sees the bullet-holed windshield and mangled front bumper and headlights they will probably call the police. *I have to get away from here.*

It's not until now that I fully realize how bad my ear is ringing. I use some spare napkins in my glove box to stuff into my ear canal and see if it's bleeding. There's no blood on the napkin but hearing out of it right now is out of the question. I take my wallet, the flower note from dad and after walking three blocks north, I call a taxi company and arrange for a car to pick me up in front of a designated restaurant. I hop in and tell the driver to take me to Astoria, Queens. He's sure to price me out first. I tell him, "I will pay whatever."

The drive is a good fifty-five minutes long and the entire ride is spent with me looking both into the past and the future. I'm worrying about my car, wondering about the people chasing me, and grieving over the prospect of having to look for another job. I imagine the men in black suits breaking into my house and rummaging through all of my belongings, looking for information on Harold Gordon. I nurse my ear with constant rubbing, a headache has developed. I fear for my life. I become angry at my father. *Why the hell is he doing this to me? He set me up and got me into this. Is he trying to show me something or is he just trying to kill me? Maybe it was payback for never amounting to all his great expectations.*

And then I turn my attention to Astoria, Queens and what I'm going to say to my brother when I see him. He won't believe me when I tell him what's happening. I haven't seen my brother in a good four to five years. He used to live in Commack and commute into the city for his job as a banker in a big glass building near Time Square. Then he moved to Queens to shorten his commute, and I've seen him about three times since then. He reminds me of the typical banker stereotype: good-looking, clean-cut, loves money and lavish things. Genetics are an interesting can of worms. My brother was always good with numbers and parties, whereas I grew up with a knack for drawing pictures and writing stories alone in my room. I'm quick to believe that the one thing he and I have most in common is our father's blue eyes.

My nerves heighten as the taxi pulls up in front of 3245 24th Street, it's a typical suburban home in Queens: two-stories with a flower basket under the big front window. I pay the fee, get out and while approaching the three-step concrete stoop, I can hear voices from inside elevate through the walls and reach the front door. My brother has a medium-low voice with a dash of arrogance. His wife, Katie, possesses a familiar, more pleasant voice to complement her personality. They're arguing about something and for a moment I hesitate to knock but this is not the time to waste any seconds. Three quick knocks seems sufficient, the voices simmer to a murmur and then footsteps grow towards the door. The door swings open and so does my brother's jaw as I'm revealed.

I softly greet him, "Hey, Joe."

It takes him a few seconds to respond… maybe he was trying to remember my name.

"Jack?" he looks back at Katie as she steps forward and smiles.

"Hey John! Come on in." She waves. My brother stops staring and steps aside. Katie leads the way to the kitchen table.

"You look great, John. It's really good to see you. Please sit down." She lowers herself into a chair and motions for me to do the same. It's only a second or two before I can see the vase in the middle of the table is not a vase at all. It's an urn. Katie notices my silent observation.

"Joe and I were just talking… your father called me last night," she confesses.

My brother's anger comes through already. "Yes and you waited until now to tell me about it!"

"Joe, I am trying to tell everybody what happened," Katie softly declares.

"Yes, out of the blue, right before my brother shows up on my doorstep you decide to tell me that you went to the funeral parlor this morning and picked up my father's ashes! And then, on top of that, you plop the old man right down on my kitchen table!" Joe always had a bit of a temper and when the mood caught him right he was completely careless with his tongue.

"Your father called me on Saturday and asked me to accept the urn. What was I going to say, no?"

"Yes, that's exactly what you say."

"Reject your dying father's wish? I was not about to do that, Joe."

Wait, what does she mean my father called her on Saturday?

"When you say he called you, what do you mean?"

Katie replies, "I mean he called, using a telephone, asking me to grant him one last favor. Listen, I know you guys were never close but the man was not an evil person."

Joe can't help but to sound condescending. "Yes and I know you visited him from time to time and that you were his closest ally so, I understand that your emotions were compromised when he called you to ask for a favor."

"Please, Joe. Just because I had compassion for *your* father, doesn't mean I'm a gullible sap."

"That's because you didn't know the man, Katie. You had no idea about who he was and what he was like."

"At least I tried," she whispers and lowers her head slowly. She doesn't want to fight right now.

I can't let go of my original question. "What do you mean he called you? He physically talked to you? Or a nurse called and spoke on his behalf?"

"No, he called me, he spoke to me."

"But when I was there the man didn't speak a word, he looked as though he was dying and lost his voice."

"He *was* dying, but he could always speak as far as I knew. Every time I visited him his health worsened, but he never lost his voice."

Joe smiles affirmatively, looking proud to have such disdain for the old man.

"See, I told you," he says. "The man was dying and didn't even have the decency to talk to his own son. He never changed. That's why I didn't go see him, that's why I *never* went to go see him; it would've been a total waste of time."

"He didn't know any better," Katie defends him. "Maybe he didn't know what to say."

I could relate to that. I didn't know what to say to him either. My eyes fall back onto the urn.

"What else do you know?" I ask.

Katie shrugs a bit, "Only that he wanted to be cremated and that he wanted me to fulfill his last wish of taking the urn and then he thanked me for everything and told me to take care of my family."

This is my cue. This is where I come in.

"The urn is not everything." I admit. "Apparently Katie wasn't his only phone call."

Joe inquires with haste, "What do you mean that's not everything?"

I reach into my jean pocket and retrieve the piece of paper. Joe reluctantly takes it from me and unfolds it. His eyes scan a few lines and when he's done reading his eyes remain in perpetual movement as he digests. Katie grabs the note from him and begins to read it herself.

"What is this?" Joe cranes his neck toward me. "What is this? When did you get this?"

"Today," I replied. "I was sent on a delivery to an office building in Holtsville. I proceeded to go into this doctor's office and tell them that I had a flower delivery for Harold Gordon."

"Who?"

"Harold Gordon. It is the name on the delivery tag. All hell broke loose after that. These men in black suits showed up in black Crown Victorias and chased me around town. They attacked me while I was inside my car. They smashed my window, put a gun to my face and threatened my life. I'm almost deaf in my left ear right now because of them, and my head is throbbing. They nearly killed me but I got away and took a taxi here as fast as I could."

"What if they followed you? You idiot, don't bring them here," Joe worries.

"But you read the letter, dad wanted me to go to that office, he knew what consequences it would bring. He wanted me to come to your house and he wants the both of us to take the urn to Montauk."

"And where in Montauk exactly?" Joe asks.

"I'm not sure." I admit. I look at Katie, "Did the urn come with another note?"

"No," Katie answers.

Joe oozes sarcasm, "No? It didn't come with instructions?"

Katie won't stand it. "Stop it, Joe. This is confusing enough."

"I'm sorry, but this is a joke. We've got an urn, a note, and no clue what to do next."

That's when the house phone rings. Joe moves to answer it. I get up and peek out the window. Putting the receiver to his ear he quietly whispers, "Hello?" Three seconds of silence and then, "Excuse me? Can you repeat that?" and then Joe puts the phone on speaker so we all can hear.

"I'm sorry sir, I said I was calling from Montauk Manor to confirm your reservation for 1:00 p.m. at Tre Bella."

Joe questions, "Who are you looking for?"

"A Mr. Joseph Miller, party of two. It's 1:15 p.m. now, sir, and I'm just calling to confirm your reservation for lunch here at Tre Bella."

For a moment, my mind goes blank on what to say next but then I snap my fingers at Joe to get his attention.

"Ask him where Montauk Manor is."

Joe leans into the phone, "And where exactly are you located?"

"We are located at 236 Edgemere Street in Montauk."

I repeat it to myself, *236 Edgemere Street... 236 Edgemere Street.*

"Who made these reservations?" Joe asks.

"Um, I believe Joseph Miller did, sir."

"Are you sure?" Joe asks.

"That is the name I have down here. Will you be honoring your reservation, sir?" The poor man seems confused.

"No," and with that, Joe hangs up and looks at Katie. "Did you do this?"

Katie shakes her head, "No."

"Did he say *anything* about this to you?"

"No, the only thing we talked about was me taking the urn."

236 Edgemere Street. I repeat it over and over in my mind.

Joe repeats over and over aloud, "This is bizarre. This is so bizarre. Jack's got a battered ear drum, the old man's sitting on my kitchen table, and I'm making phantom reservations on the opposite end of the island."

"But Joe," Katie says tenderly. "Your father wants you to go to Montauk."

This was clear. That is where we have to go next. I begin to get up out of my chair, however, Joe's not so quick to agree.

"I don't care. Why should we drop everything and all of a sudden care? Do you hear yourself? The man's crazy. He obviously owed somebody a shit-ton of money and now he's got them chasing after Jack. This isn't some great big treasure hunt; this is the old man's real life problems! Can't you see that he's putting our lives in danger? Dying wasn't enough, this is his last act and this is how he totally messes with our heads. He wants to have us running around Long Island like a bunch of fools."

Joe stops for a brief thought and then-

"And how did he get our phone number?"

Unashamed, Katie answers. "Well of course he has our phone number. I shared numbers with him, I shared pictures with him. That's what we did when I visited him. You always knew I was visiting him, Joe. I tried to be a friend to him. It wasn't easy, yes he was aloof at times, but he was never rude to me."

Joe keeps shaking his head. He refuses to put our father's name in his family tree. His stubborn nature that he uses to separate himself from our father is actually the trait that they most shared.

"So, because he was never rude to you that made you feel special? This is a sick joke, that's all."

I can definitely align with Joe's feelings and speculations. I didn't know my father well enough to rule out mental insanity or degenerate gambling debts. We spent our entire childhood and adolescence with the man, but we couldn't tell you anything about his favorite hobbies or past events. *But, this constant ringing in my ear.* It hurts me, and the ringing triggers images inside my mind. Guns, train tracks and black suits accompanied by the smell of rubber burning, gun powder and flower petals. The recent events that transpired intertwine with this current debate and I can feel myself getting dizzy and sick. I speak up.

"Joe, you didn't see these men that were chasing me. They don't work for some loan shark. They don't want to just talk about Harold Gordon and then leave peacefully."

"Then why couldn't the old man just be a normal person and tell us what the hell it is that he wants to tell us?!"

"Like Katie said, communication was not his strength. Honestly, it's not any of ours."

Joe rolls his eyes. "Well, I'm not interested in playing his game. I buried that man years ago."

Katie jumps in, "Joe! Stop talking like this. You're angry, yes, but don't be heartless."

"Well I certainly won't be brainless! This is crazy! What's going to happen? We are going to go to Montauk and spread his ashes and then what? What the hell's going to happen to us? Jack, if what you say is true and these men are after you then we need to call the police!"

I confess, "I think that is a good idea."

Joe proudly gestures in agreement.

I go on, "But we have to think this through. Maybe they *are* the police, I don't know."

"But…" Katie adds. "Even if you stop them from chasing you, it won't solve this… riddle."

That's exactly the point," Joe says, "I don't want to solve any riddles! I have a job and a wife and a house. I don't want to leave them to go play games!"

But Katie has a point and the yelling and ringing in the room and in my ear makes me desperate to get moving.

I speak in a sincere tone to reduce the volume level. "Joe, I don't know what's going on and I have no problem calling the police and telling them everything but, you weren't there. You didn't experience the chase. You weren't running for your life. And you didn't see the look in the doctor's eyes when he heard the name Harold Gordon. There's something going on and maybe you have everything going well for you here but I have no choice. These men know where I work and they know where I live and I have nowhere else to go… like the note says, I 'can't stop.'

Joe looks down at the ground for answers. Katie softly speaks up.

"For the last two years since your mother died I have visited your father more times than anybody else. We never talked about deep topics or life-changing events but, we talked. Yes, he was complex and introverted. I could always tell that there was more behind the eyes than he ever physically talked about. Even I wanted to find out more about him. But he rarely opened up… Except now. Now he is ready to talk…"

Oh, for a boy, the longed prospect of his father wanting to finally speak to him. Joe submissively rubs his face like a worn out mediator.

Katie concludes, "I will go stay with my mother for now if you are worried about my well-being. Go with your brother. Go find whatever is out there. Call the police, tell them everything that has happened and then just… go…"

Joe is silent for a moment; it's a rare occasion. He's a stubborn man but I know that he is also very cerebral. The questions that have been constantly swirling inside my mind are certainly swirling inside his. And, like me, he's got an itch. It is something that won't let this moment just sit on a shelf. There is the prospect of finally scratching this itch and quieting the questions.

The quiet moment passes as he sighs and his lips slightly part, "Don't forget the urn."

Chapter 3: Go East

Within ten minutes, Katie is out of the house and on her way to her mother's where she will stay until Joe calls and tells her it's okay to come home. Five minutes after her departure, Joe and I are pulling out of his driveway in his 2012 BMW with a suitcase full of his clothes for both me and him and a backpack to carry the urn in. It's the first time I've physically been this close to my brother since... I can't remember when. My father sits on the floor in front of me between my feet. We're one big happy family again. Joe's the first to speak, and he does so as soon as we get onto the Cross Island Expressway.

"Call the police and explain the situation."

He continues to drive as I pull out my phone and dial 9-1-1. I nervously await for somebody to answer.

"9-1-1 what is your emergency?" the operator promptly asks.

I swallow. "Hello, I'd like to report an incident."

"What is your location, sir?"

"I'm in the car right now but it's a past incident that I want to report, not something that's going on at this moment."

"What happened, sir?"

"Well, this may sound weird but I was chased by these men. You see, at first I delivered these flowers to this office building in Holtsville, and then all of a sudden the doctor must've called upon these men who were driving black Crown Victorias and wearing these suits."

I lower the phone and cover the mouthpiece so that I can think out loud to Joe.

"The suits, the cars… it could be the government."

I can hear the faint voice of the operator on the phone, "Hello? Hello?" she echoes. I raise it back to my ear.

"Hello."

"Hello, sir, you were saying that you were chased by men in suits?"

"Yes, yes I was."

"And you said that this was in Holtsville, sir?"

"Yes, in an office building."

"And where are you now, sir?"

I'm not sure what to say next.

"And where are you now, sir?" she repeats.

I cover the mouthpiece again.

"Where should I say we are?" I ask Joe.

"Tell her that you will soon be on the Long Island Expressway," Joe answers.

"But I don't want them to come and look for us, I just want to figure out who chased after me."

Joe asks, "So you just want to report the incident and say, 'okay, thank you, goodbye?' That's useless."

"I want to tell them what happened and see what they say."

Joe notes, "You just told her what happened and she said, 'and where are you now?'"

"But what if the people who tried to hurt me are the same people that I'm calling to help me?"

Joe sighs, "You're really worried about this, huh?"

"I'm not making this up, Joe. I'm just as confused as you but we have to be careful about this."

We both take a moment. I can hear the operator constantly searching for my voice on the other end of the receiver. "Hello... hello, sir... are you there?"

Then Joe squeezes my arm like a dog bite.

"I got it. Tell them that you're currently on the Long Island Expressway." I shake my head no, but he insists. "Jack, just trust me. We'll try and see if we can figure this out."

The operator continues to talk in the distance.

I raise the phone to my ear again. "Hello?"

"Yes, hello sir, are you okay?"

"I'm here."

"I said, where are you now, sir?"

"Me? I'm in my car driving on the Long Island Expressway."

"What exit are you near?"

I look at Joe and he silently mouths, "the thirties."

"I'm not sure, I'm somewhere in the thirties." I say.

"In which direction are you going?"

I pause before I finally answer. "I'm heading west toward Manhattan. I'm going into the city."

"What kind of car are you driving?"

"A silver, Toyota Avalon." For a moment I wonder if I'll ever see my car again.

"Okay, sir, what you are going to do now is pull over at the next exit and tell me which number exit it is

46

that you're at. Then you will stay right there on the side of the exit ramp and wait for the police to arrive. They will take down your full report. Okay, sir?"

Joe shakes his head no.

I break the news to the operator. "No. I'm not pulling over or stopping. I'm heading into Manhattan to see my friend. Can't you take down my full account of the incident right now?"

"Sir, if you pull over onto the shoulder of the L.I.E., then I can send a car out to take care of you."

No, we can't stop and meet up with the police but maybe we can see what they're intentions are. I can tell her that we'll meet one cop car at a designated location.

I talk into the phone. "Miss, I need one cop car to meet me at the diner off exit 37 on the North Service Road." I know the area.

Joe looks at me affirmatively and holds up his two hands and blinks all five fingers while simultaneously mouthing the word, 'minutes.'

"I will be there in twenty minutes," I tell her and then hang up.

I watch Joe get off the Cross Island Expressway and merge onto the Long Island Expressway to head eastbound toward Montauk.

Joe piggybacks on the plan, "Okay so we will drive by, survey the scene and see if anything looks suspicious."

I add, "We may not be able to find out all the answers but maybe we can figure out whether we're alone in all of this."

I look over at Joe to see if he has genuinely understood the weight of this situation.

"Let me get this straight," Joe begins, "you walk in to deliver flowers to a doctor's office?" Nope, I can tell he's still trying to wrap his mind around it.

"Yes," I answer.

"And because of the name on the tag, all of this happens?"

"Yes."

Joe checks his sideview mirror before speaking up again. "Is that your job now, flower deliveries?"

Ah, there it is. The classic Miller family showering of judgement washing over me.

"Yes." I look over at him to see his reaction. A condescending smile or a sympathetic sigh perhaps. He remains the same. A perfect poker face, but he continues to pry.

"What happened to your other delivery job... the food one?"

"You mean when I delivered food to nursing homes for that wholesale food company?"

"Yeah, that one."

"That was a long time ago. I haven't worked there in years."

"Really?"

"Really. I quit that job years ago for a job at a travel agency."

"A travel agency? Doing what exactly?" Not more than thirty minutes into the car ride, and I can see that he's already disappointed with my last five years.

I can feel my throat begin to close with hesitation but I squeeze out, "customer service."

"I thought you wanted to be a writer or something along those lines. Whatever happened to that?" He's building his throne with each subtle question.

"I don't know."

"You used to write stories and those screenplays all the time. Mom said they were good."

That wasn't a question but I know he was waiting for a response.

"Yeah," is all I give him.

"So what happened to working at the travel agency then?"

Shame and pride simultaneously battle within me and I refuse to tell him everything.

"I just don't work there anymore."

"Why not?" he asks.

"Because I don't."

"You have a Bachelor's in English Literature, right?"

"Correct."

"Did you ever think about teaching?"

"I never did until everyone began to ask me that same exact question."

I scratch my nose, he combs his hair with his hand. We drive on for about ten more minutes without saying anything until he breaks the heavy silence.

"I wonder what Katie is doing."

"Katie is going to be alright," I hope.

Joe's response of silence tells me that he doesn't completely believe my words either.

"Here we go," exit 36 comes into focus ahead. Joe wiggles in his seat and sits up. "I'm going to get off here and drive to 37 on the South Service Road, make a left and come up from behind the diner. If everything looks kosher then we will stop."

"Just like that?" I wonder.

He shrugs, "I guess so. I've never done anything like this before."

Joe does exactly as he says and in about four minutes we are slowly approaching the diner. Silent anticipation fills the cabin of the car. I'm not sure what the hell it is we are doing. *This isn't going to work; this isn't even a good plan.* But I can't think of any other option and the car rolls on. The outline of a police cruiser up ahead causes Joe to lightly pump the brakes. I slump in my seat and put my hand up to my face as if I were rubbing my forehead. My eyes are fixed on the distance through the gaps in my fingers. The police car comes into full focus.

"One police car, just as they said. Should I stop?" Joe asks.

"No, drive-by first."

He touches the gas a bit and we pass by the cop car with full intent to make a U-turn and drive by again… until I see two men sitting in a car on the side of the road. My eyes scatter the area some more and I notice two men sitting on a bench, holding up newspapers, wearing blue suits. Joe slows down to make the U-turn.

"Hold on. Keep driving, keep driving."

"What?" he inquires.

"Keep going, don't turn around."

"Why? What happened?"

"I don't know yet. It's just…" I keep looking back at the men on the bench.

"Just what?"

"It's just that something feels a bit off. Pull into this shopping center right here on the right."

Joe slowly coasts into the lot and finds a spot to park.

"What's going on? What'd you see?"

I openly wonder aloud, "If you were a man wearing a blue suit, reading a newspaper, wouldn't you have some sort of briefcase with you? I mean, why are you wearing the suit in the first place? Most likely it's work-related, right? So where's your suitcase or a bag of some sorts?"

Joe plays devil's advocate. "Maybe I'm on my lunch break, and I left it in the office or I just didn't bring one today."

It's a valid point but I contemplate further.

"But what office is there around here? There's no office building in sight. Plus, it's not just one man but two men doing the same exact thing."

"Maybe there's a law office nearby, maybe they drove here and left their suitcases in their cars. Besides, I thought you said they were wearing black suits."

"They were, but, I suppose they're not that stupid, right?"

"So what do you want to do?" Joe asks.

"Good question. I know that I don't want to go into that diner. Keep the car parked here for a moment."

I slump down in my seat to think.

I want to know who. That's it. Who are these people? The problem is I can't just go up to them and ask. They are not messing around about whatever it is that's going on. I don't know what it's going to take to stop them. *Maybe I'll go walk around to take a better look.*

I look behind my seat.

"What do you need?"

"A hat or something."

"I have a sweatshirt back there."

"That'll do."

He reaches back and presents a rolled up sweatshirt. I take it and put it over my head and lastly, I pull the hood over me so that it's barely covering my eyes.

"You're not going to go walking around out there are you?"

"Have you thought of anything else? I mean, we literally rolled into this situation with a shitty plan so, what else do you want me to do?"

Joe jokes, "A man wearing a hoodie during the middle of the day in eighty -degree weather... now *that's* not suspicious or anything." And then Joe indirectly provides insight into what to do next when he says: "You're going to look like a terrorist."

And that's when the thoughts of desperation are drowned out by the loud ringing of a bell inside my head.

I look to my left to see a young man about ten yards away getting out of his car and entering into a hardware store. He wears a long sleeve orange shirt and a dark five o'clock shadow. This was a sign. I squeeze my cell phone out of my pocket as fast as I can. On the keypad, for the second time in one day, I dial 9-1-1.

It takes one ring before the strong male voice answers. "9-1-1, what's your emergency?"

"Hello, I'd like to turn myself in." Joe's neck snaps in my direction. "I've done something terrible. I've planted explosives on myself."

"I'm sorry, you said that you've planted explosives on yourself, is that correct?"

"Yes, and I'm threatening to detonate them if my demands are not met. I was supposed to meet a cop in the diner to give my account of an incident, but now I've decided that I'm not going to play nice anymore." As I'm speaking I realize that we can't hang around here any longer, so I signal to Joe to put the car in reverse and get the hell out of this parking lot. "I was driving a Toyota

Avalon, but I ditched it and walked into the shopping center on Old Country Road. The one by the post office. I've got information, very important information and I need to talk to somebody quickly or else. I'll be inside the hardware store. I'm wearing an orange shirt with long sleeves. You have three minutes."

I hang up the phone and take a breath. When I look over at Joe the expression on his face is one of absolute shock. By now, we have left the parking lot and are beginning to drive back toward the Long Island Expressway. We hit a red light about twenty yards down the road. A pick-up truck slowly rolls up alongside of us in the 'right turn' lane. I lower my window and discretely throw my cell phone into the back of the truck's bed. It doesn't make a sound. Joe and I then hear a commotion behind us and we crane our necks to look back into the parking lot. Like a flock of pigeons descending upon the last piece of bread on earth, car doors fly open and in the span of ten seconds about ten men in suits swarm the hardware store.

And then it becomes official. A man in a black suit can be seen about fifteen yards in front of our car running toward the parking lot but on the other side of the road. He looks down the street in both directions before running across the road. I slump even deeper into my seat as the man crosses about five yards in front of the hood of our car. As he passes, the bottom of his jacket flaps upward to reveal what I had deeply suspected and feared: A badge. Harold Gordon was not some schmuck who owed a big debt to a group of thugs who were just looking to collect on his head. These thugs were finer dressed.

Joe and I lock eyes.

"Do you believe me now?" I ask.

"It can't be true."

He doesn't want to believe it. Neither do I, yet, here we are.

"Believe it or not, just keep driving."

The light turns green and we take off with controlled haste. I watch the pick-up truck turn right and head on its own way.

"What the hell is going on?" Joe asks.

"That's the million dollar question," I answer.

"What now?"

"There's nothing else to do except keep driving to Montauk."

And with that, we both mutually understand that our constant questioning of current events will not solve anything right now. We just have to stay on the path and keep our eyes open for the next clue or sign. For about an hour and a half not a single word is spoken inside the car. I can hear Joe thinking, but he doesn't share his thoughts aloud and so I keep mine quiet as well.

We head east.

I hold a steady glance outside the window as I watch the Long Island landscape shift from shopping malls and suburban neighborhoods to more dirt roads and rural farm land. Long Island has a healthy array of topography. Every twenty minutes or so I'd look into the sideview mirror and watch the cars behind us to see if I could notice if anybody was following.

As we get near our destination Joe breaks the silence. "When we get there, what are we going to say? Let's get our story straight."

"Well, I guess we just go in there and see if we can check into a room," I say.

"But what about the restaurant?" he wonders. "They were the ones who called in the first place."

"We can go in there and take a look around for sure, sit down and get a drink but, I don't think the restaurant is our next destination. Why make a reservation and never tell anyone about the reservation? He must've known that we were going to miss the reservation."

"But he must have known that they were going to call us to see if we were coming," Joe counters.

I add, "And he could've easily told them to call us to remind us. Thereby ensuring that we were told, in so many words, to go to Montauk Manor. So to make sure we would get out there by tonight-"

"You make an early reservation at the restaurant and tell them to call you," Joe finishes.

The top of Montauk Manor comes into view as we climb a great hill that is the entrance driveway. When the ground flattens out we roll through the gravel and around the luxurious property until we approach the front of the mansion.

Joe puts the car in park, stares at the marvel of human architecture and utters aloud, "I don't think I'm going to make it back in time for work tomorrow."

Chapter 4: Montauk Manor

'Elegantly old' is the best way I can describe the look of Montauk Manor. The history of the place is evident. More impressive is the way it feels. The events of the past linger in the walls and their vibrational history can be felt in my bones. It's welcoming, like a place you've visited many eras ago in past lifetimes.

We're greeted with great big smiles as we approach the front desk. One particular hotel clerk assumes her position at the nearest computer and makes direct eye contact with us.

"Hello, and welcome to Montauk Manor," she says.

Joe nods. "Hello, do you have a room reserved for Joseph Miller?"

The clerk taps on the keyboard in front of her a few times and smiles. "Yes I do, sir. Two queen-sized beds."

"What's the name on the credit card that it's reserved under?" Joe wonders.

She plays with the computer mouse. "A Carl Miller, sir."

Joe turns to me in amazement. "Well, I'll be damned."

"Would you like to use another card or do you want to use the one we have on file?"

This is a no-brainer for Joe. "The one you have on file will do just fine, thank you." He gives a big cheesy grin.

We wait the customary amount of time for the receptionist to get our room cards ready. I soak up the hotel lobby scene with its white-columned archways and wooden ceiling. Before we make our way up to our room I head into the lobby store and buy a toothbrush and deodorant. Once we swing open the door to our room we can see that it's modernized, clean, spacious, and decked out in white paint and wood furniture. I sit on the nearest bed and watch my brother place his luggage on the floor and sit down on the other bed. He takes his phone out of his pocket.

"Do you think it's safe to call Katie?" Joe asks me.

"Honestly, I don't know. Let's wait a day."

"And what are we waiting for exactly?"

"I say we go and check out Tre Bella and see if anything stands out to us."

He combs his eyebrows with his left thumb. "I need a shower and a drink," he concludes.

Then he slowly takes his shoes off one by one, picks them up and carries them to the foot of his bed.

I slip the backpack I'm carrying off my shoulders and gently carry it to the table in the kitchen area.

"Please don't put that there," Joe protests.

"Why?" I ask.

"Just put it in the corner or something."

"Why?" I repeat.

"Because it's just weird, okay. I don't want to look at it."

"Why?"

"Don't start, please," he says.

I take the backpack to the foot of my bed and gently put it down.

"Can I borrow those shorts you packed?" I ask as I begin to untie my shoelaces and unbutton my pants.

Without a word, Joe reaches into the suitcase and throws me a pair of shorts. I put them on and sit on the bed. It's just me and Joe. For the first time since I was about ten years old, we are sharing a room. He hurries to undress down to his boxers and then disappears into the bathroom and turns the shower water on.

A less intense but constant ringing still resides in my left ear. I look down at the backpack that is carrying the urn inside. It still hasn't sunk in yet that dad was officially gone. When the news was first broken to me I didn't find any closure that night nor did I come to grips with the finality of it all. I just replayed memories of the past over and over in my head. I relived situations that only contained the opportunities of regret.

I wonder if my brother did the same thing. I wonder if he has any memories of our past that he constantly replays in his mind. Carl Michael Miller was a man ingrained in our psyche, how could he not be? His impression is not something that can easily be forgotten or erased. Joe and I may have taken different paths since we left the Miller household, but the foundations on which we built our own houses are made with the same memories of the way our father treated us.

I hear the water shut off. *How long had I been listening to the clatter of my thoughts?*

The bathroom door opens up and Joe appears with a towel wrapped around his waist.

"So, are you thirsty?" he asks.

"Yeah."

"You're not going to walk into the restaurant looking like that, are you?"

I look down at myself, "What's wrong with this?"

"First off, that shirt has been through way too much today. I can smell it from here."

"Screw you, I was chased-"

"Yes, I got that. And when was the last time you actually ran before that? When was the last time you've actually, you know, broken a sweat?"

I look closely at him to make sure he's kidding before I get pissed off. He continues.

"And those shorts-"

"The shorts are yours, asshole."

He cracks a smile. "You ready to go downstairs?"

"I don't know, is this acceptable?" I mock.

"Here, put this on." He digs into his suitcase and pulls out a pair of jeans and a clean white t-shirt. I hold out my hands to catch them in case he throws them but he walks over and places them on my bed next to me. "Don't spill any drinks on the clothes."

Off the lobby floor and down a hallway is the entrance to Tre Bella. When we first walk in there is a bar to the left with a few people sitting at it. Joe takes the last stool all the way on the right hand side and I sit to his left.

"How are you gentlemen doing today?" the bartender asks as he passes out coasters.

Joe chuckles. "We will definitely be needing a few drinks after today's events."

"Well, drinks we have. What can I get you guys?" He wipes down the area of the bar in front of him and then places the white towel underneath the bar, out of site. Joe wastes no time in deciding what he wants.

"I'll have Grey Goose and soda."

"Okay," the bartender turns to me, "and for you?"

"I'll take a scotch on the rocks."

"Whoa," Joe teases.

"What kind of scotch would you like, sir?" the bartender asks.

"The house scotch is fine, thanks."

Joe makes a face. "House scotch? It's probably motor oil."

All these years and he continues to give me a hard time. Old habits die hard.

"Just drink your Grey Goose and relax, alright." I answer.

"I'm actually proud of you," he says. "You've finally learned how to drink like a man. I remember when you liked Coors Light."

"Yeah well..."

I don't have a good comeback for him. I used to drink Coors Light when I was a young man and I had the world at my fingertips. Now, I need scotch.

The bartender fixes Joe's drink first and then finishes mine a few seconds later. Both drinks are placed down in front of us. Joe picks his glass up first and uses it to quickly tap mine. A subtle cheers that feels routine before he takes a deep gulp. I follow suit and make sure to swallow just as much as he does.

There's a tiny T.V. up in the corner of the bar that catches Joe's attention.

"I hate people," he confesses after watching the monitor for five seconds. "They can't get anything right. Look at this," he motions up to the T.V. screen. "I can't believe that people would actually believe a thing that this politician says. They're absolute idiots."

My brother always had an opinion and was never shy to share it. I usually just sat back and watched.

"There's not one thing he's going to do that's going to make us better off." He looks at the bartender for reassurance.

"He's a politician; they're all crooked," the bartender says.

"It's incredible how stupid people can be, I don't understand it. I deal with stupid people all day in my line of work. And that's just the people I work for, don't get me started on the people I work with. If I drop a folder on your desk in the morning and tell you that I need the contents of that folder to be reviewed by the afternoon then when I turn around don't let me find you in the break room eating cupcakes that were left over from Sally Rottencrotch's birthday. You gotta show me that you're willing to put the work in. You gotta show me some sacrifice, some integrity, you know? But people don't think like that. Everybody wants to eat the cake but nobody is willing to learn how to bake it for themselves."

The bartender doesn't have any practiced one-liners to respond with and all I can think to do is take another gulp of my cocktail. Getting into a discussion about our day jobs is not something I want to do.

Joe looks back at the T.V. screen.

"Wow, and look at this." He reads the story off of the monitor: "Man abuses baby because girlfriend wanted to break up with him." He shakes his head. "What drives people to do something like that? I don't get it." Now, he gulps his cocktail.

An older gentleman wearing a sports jacket and fashioning a beard sits down next to my left.

"How are you doing today, sir?" the bartender asks the newcomer.

"Just fine, thank you," the older gentlemen answers.

"What can I get you?"

"A Stella, please."

Joe doesn't notice the gentleman to my left because he's wrapped up in the images on the T.V. screen. He reacts aloud to what he's watching.

"The Mets won last night? Nice, I didn't get a chance to see the highlights. Oh wait, they're going to show them right now."

This excites me. I didn't see the events of the game either. Joe and I both sip our cocktails before I sit up straight on my stool and watch eagerly as Steven Matz strikes out a batter on a curveball.

"Nasty," the gentlemen to my left replies to the pitch itself.

We watch Ahmed Rosario get a base hit up the middle and a run scores.

"He's so good," Joe murmurs.

We watch as Michael Conforto stands in the batter's box and is fooled on a curveball but still hits the ball long and far over the centerfield fence.

"Holy cow!" Joe turns to me, I smile at him. "Did you see how he hit that?" he asks.

"Yes," I say. Michael Conforto is one of my favorite players. "He's legit, man, I've always thought that about him. He's strong and he has a sweet swing."

Joe agrees. "You bet he's strong, he hit that ball over the fence with what looked like one hand. On a curveball nonetheless! How did he do that?!"

Joe's question is a bit rhetorical but the man to my left takes no time in answering. "Fundamentally? It's physics."

Joe looks at him funny and laughs him off but it doesn't stop the gentleman.

"I believe everything about the act of hitting a baseball is fundamental physics."

Joe peers at him. "Are you some sort of physicist or just a science junkie?"

"I'm a physics teacher."

I was never the kind of person who was quick to begin a conversation with a total stranger, but there are a breed of people out there who act this way. They do exist and this man was one of them. I don't have any sort of problem with them, they fascinate me actually. I guess I secretly envy their ignorance.

"A teacher? That's cool," I try to be nice to the man.

Joe points his finger sideways at the man. "You think Michael Conforto knows anything about physics? No, he's just a strong athlete."

The man ignores Joe. "His strength is a result of his proper use of energy. His strength, essentially, is energy. Maybe he never took a physics class in his life but to have a successful baseball swing you have to perform proper energy transference."

"I haven't had enough liquor for this," Joe says. "What do you shoot, mister?"

"Whiskey is fine," the gentleman answers.

Joe holds three fingers up to the bartender. "Three Jameson shots, please."

The gentleman continues, "You see, the short of it is this: the baseball swing is comprised of potential and kinetic energy."

Joe interrupts, "Where do you teach?"

He makes sure to finish his Grey Goose and soda before the shots come.

"Stony Brook University. I'm just taking a little vacation out here to recharge my atoms. Sorry, bad physics joke."

I snicker at his awareness of his own corniness. The three shots arrive.

"Just in time," Joe notes, and we all hold up our glasses to the sky.

"A toast," says the gentleman. "To physics!"

"No, no, no," Joe protests.

The man counters, "Now, now, I understand it's a heavy and intimidating subject but physics in a nutshell is easy; it's the study and analysis of how the universe behaves."

I must admit that the subject matter did intrigue me. I can't help but actually want to hear what this man has to say, preferably without the jokes though.

Joe is not so smitten. "I don't understand, is that supposed to make me okay with your toast? How about since here we are sitting in a little bar on the end of an island talking about physics and the Mets in the same sentence, let's toast to odds or chance encounters. Being a physicist and no stranger to math, you can appreciate the odds, can't you?"

"I will drink to this moment for sure. Call it chance or synchronicity it doesn't matter. It is here and so are we, so, let's cheers."

For a moment, we all can agree on something, so we throw the whiskey back into our throats.

"Let's get another Grey Goose and soda and another scotch on the rocks," Joe reorders.

"Now, back to Michael Conforto," the gentlemen says. Joe groans, and I grin at both Joe's displeasure and the man's passion. "When the pitch is thrown and by the time Michael recognizes that it's a curveball, his lower body has already begun to take its potential energy and transform it into kinetic energy. But now his hands, his hands are the key. You see, they haven't moved; they maintain their potential energy by not moving forward until the last moment when the curveball reaches the 'hitting zone.' So, his whole lower body and hips shifted forward as he lunged, but his hands stayed back; potential energy and all. So now, he has enough potential energy in his hands to turn into kinetic energy for his swing."

"And it's enough to hit the ball over the fence?" I ask.

"Precisely."

"But he has to be a strong boy to do that as well," Joe adds.

"Again, essentially, strength is energy."

Joe squints, "You always talk to people like this?"

"Anyone who will listen," he answers.

"What's the most common question they all ask you?" I ask.

He answers without missing a beat, "Why did you want to become a physicist?"

"And you tell them?"

"Because of the wonder."

"The wonder?" Joe doesn't seem enthused.

"The wonder of it all. It's all so spectacular, intriguing and peculiar all at the same time, and I've been crazy enough to think that I can figure it all out."

"Do you believe someday you will?" I ask.

"Not a chance," he laughs. "But, the more I teach it and the more I talk about it, the more I think that I'm not supposed to figure it all out, nor would I be disheartened if I don't. I've simply become content in unraveling the gracious layers of the wonder. I mostly teach it, but I also get some time to head out to some really cool places where they are doing some great experiments and creating new theories and it's just the nature of seeking that I enjoy. The reward is in the work, as they say."

A moment of silence for his moment of honesty. I haven't found much reward in my work, but I'll be damned if I take this moment away from this man.

I try to keep the conversation going with the first question that comes to mind. "So being the first physicist

I've ever met face to face, I feel compelled to ask you one question in case I never get another chance."

"Go on," he says.

"Does physics offer up a theory as to the point of the universe?" It's a constant question that I have never been able to shake. It hides in plain sight sometimes. I always look for its answer; a reason.

"The point of the universe?" he asks.

"Well you said, in short, physics was the study of the universe. So, I was wondering if it offered a theory on the reason the universe exists in the first place."

The gentleman sneaks a smiles out of the corner of his mouth. "As to the existence of the universe and *how* it came about, there are theories, yes. As to *why* it came about? Your guess is as good as mine."

He widens that smile to include his whole mouth.

"So you've got nothing for us in 'the meaning of life' department?" Joe asks.

"Would it blow your mind if I told you that everything was nothing?"

Joe is quick with his quip, "Coming from you that would not surprise me."

"What I mean is, if you take everything: people, animals, rocks, desks, glass… everything… and look at it closely, layer under layer, closer and closer, what you will find is energy acting as atoms with electrons swirling around protons and neutrons. Which, are made up of smaller particles called quarks. And at the heart of all these particles and atoms and protons and neutrons and electrons and quarks and everything else is: energy. The substance of everything is energy and at the most fundamental core of energy is: nothing. At the center of energy is just… space. So, in a sense, 'substance' is a bad word… It's more like 'essence.' The essence of everything is this unexplained nothingness."

"Do you have a name for this nothingness?" I ask.

"Many people have different names. I call it 'the wonder'," he says.

"Three more shots of Jameson!" Joe shouts.

"And then I must be going. I have to meet my wife for dinner," the gentleman says.

I can't help but be channeled into a state of mind. It's a state where I'm not sure what I'm thinking about. I'm just sort of... stunned. Stunned and confused by the man's explanation. And in being stunned and confused I have no answers nor explanations, only questions.

The gentleman concludes, "So even we are layers built on top of the wonder. Products of the wonder while simultaneously connected to the wonder."

Joe tries to come to his own conclusion. "So then, if everything is essentially nothing, the meaning of it all is..."

The first word that comes to me that finishes his sentence is the word 'nothing.'

But the gentleman says something else. "Then the meaning is whatever you want it to be."

The shots show up and Joe and the gentleman grab theirs first before I take mine and join them in raising it above our heads.

"What shall we toast to this time?" Joe asks.

"I went already," replies the gentleman.

Joe takes the reigns. "To Michael Conforto!"

And we all smile and cheers each other.

"Well, men, it's been a pleasure. Thanks for the moment." And with that he throws some money on the bar top and shakes our hands; out of our lives as quickly as he joined in.

Joe and I sit for a moment and work on our cocktails. My stomach growls.

"I think we should be moving along as well," I tell Joe.

"You don't want another one?" he asks.

"I'm a little hungry."

"Well, we are in a restaurant."

"I know but, do you feel like we are supposed to find anything here?" I ask.

"Maybe we need to look around," Joe says.

We turn around on our stools. The place is relatively empty with only a few tables occupied by couples in typical upscale vacation clothes. That's it. Joe turns to the bartender.

"Excuse me, did anyone leave a message for Joe Miller?"

"Um, not with me, no."

Joe tries again. "What about Jack Miller?"

He shakes his head. "Nope."

Last try. "What about Harold Gordon?"

"No messages were left with me. Are you expecting one?"

"I don't know." And with that, Joe turns his attention back to his cocktail. "I'm not going to go fishing for something and make a fool out of myself in the process." He tilts his head back along with the rest of his drink. Then he pulls out his wallet and puts some cash on the bar. I reach into my pocket but he stops me. "That covers both of us. Just finish up, and we'll get going."

I take a healthy gulp of scotch, blow my cheeks out, wince and repeat until my glass is empty in quick time. My ear doesn't bother me as much anymore.

Joe compliments my efforts, "Not bad."

"I've been practicing."

We stand and walk out.

As soon as the elevator doors close us in, Joe blurts out, "Damn that was a bizarre conversation, huh?"

"Interesting, to say the least."

A beat of silence.

"What do you want to eat?" Joe asks.

"I'll have to take a look at the menu."

"You know what the best part about ordering room service is, right?" he asks.

"What?"

"The room's under dad's card. So I'm going to go nuts on this room service charge."

"We should've charged the drinks to the room," I say.

"Oh shit, let's go back!" he jokes.

We both laugh. As crazy as our current life situation is right now, for a moment it feels 'okay' in a way. Together, we are heading back to our room with bellies full of liquor and nothing else on our plate then to eat and hang out. It's been a while since I've eaten dinner with somebody else.

The elevator doors open and our room is no more than a ten second walk to the left. Opening the door and entering, I plop down on my bed and take a deep breath.

Joe gets the room service menu. "Let's see what they got."

"You want to watch T.V.?" I ask and sit up to search for the remote.

"Sure… Katie hates when I try to watch T.V. during dinner."

"Really?"

"Yeah, then again, Katie hates a lot of things I do."

He sits down on the couch in front of the television.

"Hates?" I can't imagine sweet Katie hating anything.

"Well, hates is a strong word. Let's just say I have a knack for disrupting the peace. I do some things that would seem inconsiderate, and she has no problem calling me out on them."

"I understand," and then I try to defend her. "That's good though, isn't it? That sort of honesty."

"Sure," is all he says.

I try to be the voice of reason, I don't know why but I do. "It's good sometimes to have that person to keep you in check, no?"

"What are you trying to say? I need to be kept in line?"

On purpose, I reply, "As a matter of fact, yes. Now don't give me any more attitude about it."

He throws up his hands, "Now you're doing it too."

He knows I was teasing, but the wit doesn't last long. His eyes go back to the menu, but his mouth keeps going.

"Probably best for the both of us that I'm out here, anyways."

I'm not sure if he's talking to me or to himself. It feels more like the latter.

"Why do you say that?" I pry.

"Ah, don't mind me." He tries to shrug it off.

But I do mind. "Are you guys doing alright?"

He takes his eyes off the menu but looks downward, not at me.

"No marriage is perfect."

It sounds like a cliché but maybe it's true, what do I know about marriages or relationships. I've had a few intimate moments with people, but they were purely physical and rarely emotional. Nothing recently. As of late I've just been trying to keep my head above water. Now that I think about it, maybe that's how it's always been; just me trying to keep my head above water.

Joe goes on without me pushing him. "She keeps pressing the issue of kids, and we're running out of time."

"Are you guys having trouble conceiving?" I wonder.

"No…"

I wait for him to say more but he seems to bite his tongue. He pretends to read the menu again.

I try to relate to his issue and try to comfort him by thinking of our own mother. "You know mom was pretty old when she had us, it's never too late."

"Sure."

It doesn't work. He's done being open and honest. Typical Miller family conversation. But, maybe it's the scotch because I feel like diving a little deeper into this moment. It's been a while since I had my brother all to myself and who knows when the next opportunity will be.

"That woman deserved the Medal of Honor," I state.

Joe lets out a small gust of air that results in a 'pfew' then affirms, "You can say that again."

Ah, mom. If dad was the strong, silent type, like an old oak tree, then mom was the constant and gentle breeze that never left you. Unlike dad, she was extroverted, some would say loud. She also never lacked a comforting word when it was needed. She was reasonable and down to earth. A hard-working mother and wife.

Joe continues on the subject, "That woman put up with more bullshit than we could've ever imagined. How she stayed with him is beyond me."

"Maybe she loved him," I contest.

"I doubt it. I think it was just more of a generational thing; she was the wife who stood by and supported her husband no matter what."

"You're making it sound like dad beat her or cheated on her and she just sat back and took it. I don't think that was the case at all. I just think she was a supportive person who cared about her family and even if she didn't understand dad all the time, she still wanted to keep her family together."

Joe agrees with a simple nod of his head. "And when she died she had a funeral like a regular, humble human being. Not a rat race like this."

His mind comes back to Carl Miller. The grooves in the record are deep and worn out. He wiggles uncomfortably on the couch after he alludes to dad. Mom is a sweet memory but the bitter thoughts of dad won't go away that easily. Literally, dad won't leave us, either. The urn sits five feet away.

I suppose his nagging presence pisses Joe off. I suppose because I can understand my brother's present state, it means I'm there in the same basket as him. Confused and angry. I feel pity for both of us because thinking of mom made us feel good if but for a brief moment. I enjoyed the memories and I search for more of those enjoyable moments. I transport back to a time in our youth before we became 'mature.' Back when we were soft and not so damn calcified. The good old days.

The memories I force myself to find are not of mom, but of dad. Some good memories of him. They aren't epic tales but rather short, spontaneous moments. I feel the urge to share this fleeting glimpse of lightheartedness with my brother.

"Do you remember when dad had you standing on top of his shoulders at Gaynor Park and you had your head in this big pine tree trying to reach the baseball I had just hit over the fence? It was my first little league homerun."

Joe remembers. "I did it because he was so adamant about getting that ball. He kept yelling, 'reach higher, just a little bit higher.'"

I remembered my exact point of reference. "I was sitting on the bench after I'd just finished rounding the bases, looking at you guys thinking, 'Yes, get it for me, please.' I wanted that ball so bad."

Joe thinks aloud, "I will say, he actually seemed to care about our sports careers I'll give him that."

I reflect, "I was going to be the next big thing. A major-leaguer. I feel like that's what he wanted most out of me. I knew dad always loved baseball more than anything. It was his passion that's for sure. If I could have just been better-"

"What? He would've paid more attention to you? Showed tender love and care toward you?" Joe clenches his jaw.

"Most of my memories, when I reach back, are of him pitching batting practice to me at some local park and you in the outfield chasing after the balls. Then all of us going to McDonald's afterwards."

Joe turns the corners of his mouth upwards. "We ate so much McDonald's."

"It was our go-to dinner of choice after any sports-related practice or game. All of us riding back from the game in the same car, eating together, talking about the game; it was like we were a real family."

Joe jumps in, "Until the morning came and the door swung open and the old man came in to wake us up for school. He wouldn't even walk into the room he'd just stand in the doorway, flick the light on and order, 'Get up, fix your bed, get dressed and do them quickly!'"

I remember that precisely. "Turning the light on was the worst part because he'd turn it on, say what he'd have to say, and then just walk out with the door open and the light still on so you couldn't go back to sleep if you tried."

"You wouldn't dare go back to sleep because you had to be dressed in three minutes and that was including the time it took for you to make your bed."

Oh, the bed-making. He was such a stickler for a properly made bed. He had a lot of rules and if we didn't comply with them he wasn't afraid to spank us on the ass or slap us in the face. He knew how to control and intimidate us. Actually, there's one occasion of mental abuse that stands out more to me than any physical beating I ever got. When Joe got older and brasher, he tried to fight back a few times but that always resulted in even more disciplining. So, when it was my turn, I just waited until I was old enough to physically distance myself from it all.

"Sporting events were his real passion," I return to the subject. "The man was a joy around the ballfield or soccer field or any kind of event where competition was present. And if I didn't hustle on every play or come home with a dirty uniform, he would have something to say about it. He'd tell me I wasn't working hard enough or I didn't care enough. It was a constant uphill climb just to get to a place where he couldn't look down on me."

Joe snaps. "Because you didn't hit thirty homeruns a year? Because you weren't Pete Rose? Please! The man was miserable, that's all. He was happy ten percent of the time when he was either at one of our sports games and we were successful or, he was drunk as a skunk and was a curmudgeon the other ninety-percent of the time."

"But if we could have done more..." I insist on trying to take responsibility for my father's ways.

"That's enough," Joe stands up and walks in a circle. "I'm starving and I want to eat." He sits back down and picks up the menu again and tries to read it. I watch as he rocks back and forth on the couch.

"I didn't ask for this. I didn't wake up this morning and ask for this," he mutters.

Was he saying that this was my fault?

"I didn't ask for this either, Joe," I insist.

"Yet, here we are, digging up shit from the past when we're supposed to be burying it."

I deflect, "Hey you had the urn, it's not like I dragged you into this. You were getting into this no matter what. He gave me the note and *you* had the urn."

Joe ignores me. "I'm ready to order." He stands up and tosses me the menu. "Pick something; we're not paying for it anyway." He walks over and picks up the room phone.

The air between us fills with that familiar feeling of heavy awkwardness. I try to break it up with a moment of levity.

"What's the most expensive item on the menu?"

Joe takes a moment then says, "Probably the surf and turf."

"Put me down for three."

It works, Joe smirks.

We order dinner and for the next forty-five minutes we watch T.V. in silence until it comes. Then we eat and make minimal conversation about how good the food is. After my last bite, I wipe my mouth with a napkin and lay back upon my bed.

I acknowledge my satisfied hunger, "That worked."

He leans back as well and for the next hour we lie on our respective beds and quietly watch T.V. again.

I blink.

When I wake up the clock says 2:30 a.m.

I look over at Joe's bed and see an outline of him under the covers. I get up to take a leak, then shuffle back to bed and try to force myself to sleep.

At 6:00 a.m. the phone rings. I rise out of bed and follow the ringing to the phone sitting next to the T.V.

"Hello?"

"Hello, Mr. Miller?"

"Yes."

"Your car is ready."

"My car?"

"Yes sir, your driver is standing here at the front desk. Your car is ready for you, sir."

"Okay, thank you."

I hang up and look at Joe who is sitting up in his bed fingering his eye.

"Get dressed, there's a car downstairs waiting for us," I tell him.

"Where's it going to?"

"That's a great question."

We say no more as we throw some clothes on and are heading toward the elevator ten minutes later. We leave with everything that we came with just in case we don't come back. I carry Joe's bag of clothes to his car, keep the backpack, and then head over to the town car that's waiting for us. Joe finishes talking to the driver and meets me behind the vehicle.

"We're going to Montauk Downs."

"The golf course?"

"Yep."

"We don't even have golf clubs."

"Maybe we're supposed to be caddies," Joe responds sarcastically.

"Very funny."

He opens the door for me and we jump in as the car pulls away from Montauk Manor.

"Montauk Downs," I repeat as we make our way down the driveway. "Have you ever played there before?"

"Several times," Joe says. "It's a great course. You?"

"Nah, never made it out here for golf. Farthest east I ever got was Island's End Golf Course, but that was a long time ago. What did you come all the way out here for?"

"A couple of co-workers were going and asked me to join."

"Are you any good?" I ask.

"Of course I am," he quickly replies.

"I remember you were an avid golfer back in the day, I guess you kept with it all this time?"

"I did. It's a great way to do business, but it's also a great way to get away from work sometimes."

"How'd you sleep last night?" I ask.

"I dreamt about Katie."

I softly nod although I can't relate.

"So, do you know where this place is?" I ask.

"Yeah, it's not far from here at all. Five minutes," he estimates.

Shortly thereafter we pull up to the front of the golf course and get out of the car. Even though the driver says he'll wait for us, I bring the backpack just in case. It's morbid slinging your father around your back, but we might need it. Maybe dad wants to be buried on the 18th green or something. I didn't know him to ever golf a day in his life but today I'm trying to prepare myself for anything. If we find out he once played a round with Ronald Reagan and Fidel Castro then I'm getting ready for it.

"This is one of the highest-rated golf courses on Long Island," Joe informs me. We enter through the front and I look around. I can't say that I'm impressed.

"Looks like a regular golf course to me."

"This is the clubhouse, I'm talking about the course itself."

"May I help you gentlemen?" A voice off to the side calls to us.

It's a woman inside a little booth.

"No, thank you," Joe quickly responds then turns to me. "Let's walk around for a little bit."

"What if we are supposed to actually walk around the course?" I speculate.

"Then that would be pretty cool but they don't let you just walk around the course. And without golf clubs we'd stick out like sore thumbs."

He leads the way as we walk straight past the pro shop and through a set of doors which lead outside to a patio area with tables and chairs and the first tee; right next to it is a booth labeled 'Starter.'

The man inside the booth, the Starter himself, calls out the next group of golfers who are scheduled to tee off on the first hole. "Hanson, group of four. Hanson, group of four, please report to the first tee."

To our right is the driving range. It inspires Joe.

"Maybe I can borrow a driver from the pro shop, get a bucket of balls and work on my slice. You know, do something productive while we're out here."

I can smell the fresh cut grass and the breeze is noticeably strong.

"Windy day for golf," I observe.

"Every time I play here it's at least 15 miles per hour or worse. That's part of what makes it such a tough course."

I wonder if maybe we should go into the pro shop and snoop around. Joe is too busy watching the swings of the golfers on the driving range.

"You see that?" he points to one left-handed golfer after he shanks the ball to his left. "That's exactly my problem, I'm sliding with my hip just like that and it's pulling my hands with me and opening up my club face at the point of contact. The frustrating thing is I know exactly what I'm doing wrong it's just taking me weeks to fix. It's such a hard sport. You gotta have a lot of respect for the guys who are really good at this sport. People think it's just about beer and cigars but it takes a lot of skill."

"To drink beer and smoke cigars?" I joke.

"To be really good at this sport." He has a look of determination as he eyes the same left-handed golfer's swing.

"It looks like elementary physics to me," I quip.

"Damn potential and kinetic energy," he replies.

"You don't find it boring?" I ask.

"It's only boring if you're not good at it."

I turn from the driving range and watch the last person on the first tee hit the ball down the fairway and then drop his club into his golf bag and drive away with the rest of his group. As they chase after their balls and drive away from us I'm reminded of how long it takes to finish eighteen holes of golf.

"It's such an investment though, isn't it?" I ask.

"What is?"

"A round of golf. It's like, four hours of your day."

"That's right, four hours of a challenge. A challenge just between you and the course."

"I remember it being so frustrating every time I played."

Joe responds bluntly, "That's because you suck at it."

I shoot him a glance; I'm not offended I just don't like the fact that he's right.

Joe finally takes his eyes off the golfers at the driving range and says, "Let's check out the pro shop; see if they got a driver I can borrow."

"You're not serious."

"Don't worry, Jack, I'll only hit a small bucket, it's not like we know what we're doing here. My guess is we're supposed to wait. And I'm not going to look like an idiot waiting out here so, I'm going to hit a few balls while we wait for something."

"Something?" How typical of Joe to try and figure out what he could personally get out of whatever was going on at that moment.

"Something, anything, maybe nothing. It will only take ten minutes," he insists.

He begins to head back inside where the pro shop is when the man in the Starter's booth announces, "Gordon, party of two... Gordon, party of two, please report to the first tee."

Joe stops in his tracks and hangs his head. Then he turns to me.

Sarcastically he mutters, "Great. Are you happy now?"

Chapter 5: Inquire

The man in the Starter's booth is a wrinkly old gentleman sporting an Air Force hat with thin white hairs creeping out from underneath the sides. Father time has curved his back and shoulders forward. When we approach the booth he has his head down as he looks over the sheet of paper that lies in front of him. It's a list of all the groups that are set to tee off today.

I approach him gently. "Excuse me, sir."

He raises his bloodshot eyes from the white sheet of paper.

"Did you say, 'Gordon, party of two'?"

He lowers his eyes back downward and fingers the sheet of paper for a moment. "Yes, Gordon, party of two, you guys are up right now."

"Does it say anything else on there about us?" I ask.

He looks back up at me. "Does *what* say anything about you?" he inquires.

I'm not sure how to explain but I'll try. "That piece of paper in front of you, or maybe there's another piece of paper with information on it that says something more about us and what's going on and stuff." I'm not doing a good job. The old man's eyes stare at my heads, all four of them. I go on, "You see, we don't have clubs but-"

"What do you mean, you don't have clubs?" he interrupts.

Joe jumps in, "We're not sure if we are supposed to be playing golf or not, we are not sure what the hell we're supposed to be doing here at all."

The old man scratches his stubble chin. "You're not sure what you're supposed to be doing at a golf course?"

Joe and I look at each other with frustration.

I run my hand once through my hair and then take a deep breath. "Does it say anything else about Harold Gordon on that sheet of paper?"

The old man with the Air Force hat drifts his bloodshot eyes my way once again. "Who?" he asks.

"Harold Gordon. That's what Gordon, party of two means. Except, we don't know what we're supposed to do with it. We don't have golf clubs to actually play, but our father did send us here for something. We're supposed to be here but we don't know what this place has to do with Harold Gordon or Carl Miller?"

The old man swallows a big lump in his throat and then echoes my father's name, "Carl Miller?"

"Yes," I tell him.

"Who are you?" he asks and squints his eyes as if we've met before and he's trying to recognize us.

"Carl Miller was our father," I tell him as I read the current look on his face. It's a mixture of extreme confusion with a touch of fear.

"And he sent you here?" The old man asks as his eyes now shift off of our faces and scan the area around us.

"Yes, right before he died," I say.

Joe jumps in again, "Did you know him?"

He says nothing, but the old man indicts himself just by the way he takes a step back and looks away.

Joe picks up on it. "You *did* know him. Well, he sent us here. Do you know why? Do you know anything about this Harold Gordon?"

"No!" the force of him raising his voice causes him to begin to cough uncontrollably for a few seconds. When he's finished he takes a rolled up napkin out of his pocket and wipes his lips. "It's time for you to go," he concludes.

"We can't go, there's nowhere for us to go, this is where we are supposed to be right now. We're here to talk to you," I tell him.

"There's nothing to talk about." And then he takes his hat off for a second to wipe his scalp down with the palm of his hand.

"Please, sir, whatever it is… we need to know. Carl Miller's last dying wish was to be buried here in Montauk."

"So then bury him and be on your way," he insists.

"But we don't know where to bury him. He didn't tell us where."

Joe's finger starts wagging at the old man. "But you knew him. That's why we are here. You knew Carl Miller. So all we need is ten minutes of your time. Ten minutes so that you can tell us something about him and we can get an idea about where to put his ashes down and then you'll never see us again. Listen, we're not trying to take up much of your time, we're just looking to get this over with."

I look at Joe as he tries to strike a deal with the old man. The old man begins to cough again so he reaches for the napkin and covers his mouth. When he settles down he wipes his mouth again and licks his lips. "Let me see some identification," he finally says.

We both hesitate for a moment. I remember that I left my driver's license back at the doctor's office so I look at Joe and gesture for him to go ahead and produce his I.D.

"Fine," he pulls out his wallet. "There you go, Joseph Miller, that's me." He hands his driver's license to the man.

The old man takes a pair of glasses out of his shirt pocket and puts them on top of his nose. He slowly inspects the I.D. before handing it back. Then he turns to me. "And where's yours?"

"Me? I didn't know I was going to need it today."

Joe tries to turn the tables. "And what about you, sir, what should we call you?"

He thinks, and then, "Just call me the Starter."

"That's it?" Joe asks.

"That's it," the old man affirms.

"Well then, what can you tell us, Starter?"

He takes a moment of contemplation. "When did your father die?"

"Recently," Joe says.

The old Starter drops his eyes down toward his white sheet again. A man in his forties wearing a perfectly ironed white-collared shirt comes up from behind us.

"Is everything alright, gentlemen?" the man asks.

Joe turns around, "Just fine, thank you."

"Let's keep the groups moving." The man says and walks away but not before he gives a firm look toward the Starter.

"You see, this is not a good time," the Starter says.

"We can't leave until you talk to us. If you don't talk to us now then we will stand right here until it becomes a good time to talk to us. All we are asking for is ten minutes, sir, that's all. Please," I beg him.

The Starter shifts around uncomfortably. He peeks around the booth and watches the white-collared man walk inside the pro shop and then he calls to a young boy passing by on a golf cart.

"Anthony!" he waves him over.

The boy stops the golf cart and runs up to the booth.

"I'm going to need a short break, can you take over for a few minutes?" the Starter asks.

"You want me to be the Starter? Bob's already busting my balls to finish washing off all the golf carts from yesterday."

"Yeah I know, he's busting my balls too, but it's only going to be a few minutes. Make that four minutes to be exact." He looks back at us to make sure we understand that he's serious about his time limit.

"I don't think that's a good idea right now," Anthony argues.

"I've been here for forty-five years so I think Bob can handle me taking four minutes, okay?" the Starter becomes agitated.

"That's easy for you to say, what if I get in trouble?"

"If Bob does anything to you then I'll show you which car out in the parking lot is his and you and your friends can put salt in the gas tank, okay? I won't be long." The old man is done negotiating and so he grunts as he steps out of the booth and walks past us and over to a patio table and takes a seat. We follow behind and sit down across from him.

"Let's make this quick. You want to know something about your father, right?"

Joe responds, "Carl Miller, yes. We want to know where to bury him."

I jump in, "And we want to know about Harold Gordon."

"I only know about Carl Miller. I can tell you a little bit about him if that will appease you, but I can't tell you where to bury him. I wouldn't know the slightest thing about that."

"That's fine," Joe agrees.

"We were quite close back then. As close as brothers could be," the Starter begins.

"Brothers?" I look at Joe.

"Not blood... even closer than that. You see, what's lost on generations nowadays is the concept of loyalty and service. It's as foreign to them as an 8-track."

I take note again of his Air Force hat. "You served together?"

"Two years together. It was him, me and another pal at that time. We did everything together along with my brother, my blood brother, who was living and working in the area at the same time."

I never knew much about my dad's service in the U.S. military. He never talked about it unless he was complaining about politics.

"Where did you guys serve?" I ask.

The Starter looks surprised and wrinkles his eyebrows. I guess he thought we would have at least known about our father's past and he seems upset now that he has to keep telling us more information.

"Right here… in Montauk," he says.

"You served in Montauk?" I question.

He takes a moment and relaxes his face muscles. "Actually, I'm not surprised he didn't talk about it. None of us did. We were the 773rd Aircraft Control and Warning Squadron in 1958 and were in the middle of being re-designated the 773rd Radar Squadron. Our base was located at Camp Hero, about five minutes down the road. That's where we ate, slept, trained and worked."

I had always assumed dad served in Vietnam or something. I was wrong.

"What exactly was the Air Force doing in Montauk?" I ask.

"I just told you. We were operating as a squadron for air data and defense. Montauk was a vulnerable piece

119

of American land that had military presence on it since the days of the American Revolution. The damn lighthouse was built to lookout for British ships. Ever since then it has housed the Army, Navy and Air Force. First it looked out for British ships then German U-boats then... Soviet communists."

The last part about communists seems to put a bad taste in his mouth and his body language changes. He tries to conclude the conversation.

"So, if I were you I'd go to Camp Hero. That's where we spent most of our time when we served out here."

His belly starts to jiggle a bit and then the movement builds up to his chest, neck and head. The back of his hand raises up to his mouth and protects us from projectile phlegm as he goes into another coughing fit.

I wait until he settles down. "And you still live here?"

"Was born on Long Island and after I served I picked up golf and stuck around Montauk ever since. A lifetime islander."

There's an awkward pause in the conversation. A moment of silence where I can feel that the old man was done telling us everything he wanted to tell us but, I can't let him go without asking again.

"And what about Harold Gordon, was he somebody that served with you guys as well?"

The old Starter slams his fist down on the table. "I told you I didn't know anything about that!"

Joe responds to the old man's aggravation with some of his own. "But clearly you have some kind of knowledge about it. What's the big deal? What's your problem?"

"It was our father's dying wish. We're just trying to get it right," I add. My goal is to make the man not want to be a hindrance to us.

"Listen to me," the old man's tone gets deep as he scolds us with his raspy voice and his stern finger. "Stick with what you know and don't try to know any more than that. Your father wants to be buried in Montauk?… then bury him in Montauk. As for me, I have nothing more to say to you fellas, nor do I ever want to see you again. Go to Camp Hero and leave me alone."

And with that, he coughs up another piece of phlegm, spits on the floor, gets up and goes back to his booth.

I shake my head. "He knows more. He knows more, but he won't tell us."

Joe tries to shake it all off. "At least we know where to bury him now."

"Camp Hero?" I ask.

"Obviously," Joe answers.

"Just because we know they were stationed at Camp Hero doesn't mean that's where dad wants to be buried. And that doesn't solve the Harold Gordon problem," I tell him.

"We can sit here and pester that old man until we are blue in the face but we won't get any more answers. Maybe there's more to find at Camp Hero."

"But I know he knows more," I insist.

Joe puts his hand on my shoulder and lowers his voice, "Listen, we'll go to Camp Hero and check it out. Afterwards, if you're still not content, then we can always come back here and put salt in the old man's gas tank."

He grins at his own jest, but it's not comforting. I'll go to Camp Hero, fine, but I'm not leaving Montauk until I find out why somebody in a black suit put a gun to my head.

Chapter 6: Camp Hero

As our car pulls away from Montauk Downs, Joe asks the driver to tell us about Camp Hero. He begins spitting out a few facts about it, some of which the old man had just told us.

"Camp Hero State Park is over 410-acres. Did you know that Montauk has been an area of military interest since the American Revolution? In World War One, the U.S. Army had airplanes and troops stationed there. During World War Two, the threat of German U-boats forced the Navy to build docks, hangers and barracks in the surrounding areas. When the war ended, the base was transformed into a training site for the Army Reserves.

During the 1950's, the Army let the Air Force move in and set up shop inside Camp Hero. No longer fighting against Nazi's, the Russians and Communists now became a subject of concern. Soviet airplanes could fly way above the range of the artillery guns that the Army had on the ground. So, the Air Force created a radar system that included a Ground Air Transmitter

Receiver facility with a giant antennae. This system would provide enhanced electronic measurements of the surrounding area. The giant antennae that the Air Force built as part of the system would be able to detect and identify approaching enemy planes."

He pauses then resumes.

"Camp Hero was built to resemble a small fishing village in case there were any spy boats looking in off the coast. The workout area or gymnasium, was built to look like a church. The guns were constructed into the side of man-made hills. Train tracks ran through heavily-wooded areas and were used to transport weapons and supplies. Eventually, the Army left completely and the Air Force officially stayed around working with the surveillance and radar system until about 1980. The antennae is still up today, but no longer works. Same with some of the Battery Dunns."

I must admit, I have lived on Long Island my entire life and I never knew about Camp Hero. I also never knew anything about my father spending the earlier part of his life serving and living in Camp Hero. When I think about my lack of knowledge, it's both intriguing and a bit embarrassing.

"Why wouldn't dad ever say a word about this place?" I wonder.

Joe shrugs. "I thought we were beyond asking 'why' questions. Let's face it, we didn't know shit about the guy. At least now we know this much."

I begin to worry. *Is this really where we are supposed to be going next? What if we don't find anything at Camp Hero and find ourselves at a dead end?*

The idea of not being in control and blindly relying on unforeseeable future events is nerve-wracking and frustrating.

Our car takes a right hand turn onto a gravel path and I can tell that we are close. We slowly proceed down the road only to eventually take another right hand turn onto a narrow dirt path. After about a half of a mile, the car stops and the driver exits and walks around the vehicle. I make eye contact with Joe. Our door opens.

The driver sticks his head in. "We've arrived, Camp Hero State Park. From where we are right here, you can walk around a bit. There's a little path right up ahead or you can go south, off the path, and check out the cliffs and ocean. Just be careful."

I grab the backpack holding the urn inside. He steps back to allow us to exit the car. The sun hits the top of my head as my eyes scan the landscape. It looks like an ordinary camping grounds: benches under trees surrounded by a concrete walking path. Around the outside of the path is brush accompanied by tall trees behind it. The further I walk away from the vehicle and the more I look around, the more relics I begin to make out in the distance. Joe begins to make his way toward one of them almost immediately. It's a big metal saucer-like structure that resembles half a giant hockey puck sticking out of the side of a hill. The structure is about twenty feet off the ground and underneath it is a brick wall painted white with big black lettering neatly spray painted on it. It's hard to make out the words but as we get closer they become clear: "CLOSED TO THE PUBLIC. DO NOT TRESSPASS."

A few feet to the side of the massive structure is a wooden post about waist high with a clear, see-through box resting on top. Inside the case is a picture of the structure in 1949 when it was in-use. The picture is a bit different from the structure that we see before us today. In the picture, next to the saucer-like structure, there is a long metal tube sticking out of the hill; it's a barrel. Above the picture is a label of what we are looking at: "BATTERY DUNN 113"

This was one of a few long range 16-inch gun barrels that stayed nestled into the side of the hill and pointed out onto the Atlantic Ocean, ready to fire. The size of the gun itself in length was just under 70 feet. Now all that was left of it was a picture, a few facts and a warning to the public to keep out.

We walk a little bit longer past Battery Dunn 113 and can see the gymnasium that's dressed up like a church. At a passing glance one would simply assume it to be a place of worship but inside used to be the inner workings of other plans and motives. We pass water pump stations and old, rusty barracks. The abandonment of the area doesn't take away from its ghostly aura. At any minute I expect the face of a young cadet to pop up inside the window of one of these structures. In a way, this place was its own little town. A little nook at the end of an island designed as the first line of defense.

Joe and I don't even talk about the towering structure that we can't miss or ignore, but it's the one that we walk towards last. It's the radar antennae that still sits above the Ground Air Transmitter Receiver facility. Although no longer working, something emanating from the antenna is coming in loud and clear. It is an undeniable structure. The information provided at the scene says the antenna weighs 70 to 80 tons and the base of the entire tower is more than 80 feet high and 60 feet long. There are several 'NO TRESSPASSING' signs hanging on the chain-linked, barbed-wire fence that surround the deserted structure.

"It's big," Joe says.

"Ya think?" I reply.

Joe chuckles to himself before putting his head down and walking on. My head can't help but continue to stay tilted upwards as I keep an eye on the ominous 'entity.'

"So now what?" Joe asks as our feet leave the concrete path and find soft soil before we enter a field of high brush and trees with only a dirt path to guide us.

"I guess we find a nice little place to do this," I answer.

I assume Camp Hero is the place that dad had in mind.

We walk deeper along this dirt path and further southeast away from the graveyard of past military technology. As we do, it becomes easier to hear the sounds of the birds. They were always there but I hadn't noticed them until now. Maybe it was the stark difference of visuals; the now green landscape is more acceptable than the rustic buildings. It's more comforting, more forgiving. The feelings of five minutes ago are not the feelings I'm experiencing right now as our feet carry us further. The singing of birds and chirping bugs are held together by the hum of the silence in between. Joe and I don't say a word.

Then, creeping back into me from the past, one caveat begins to develop again. My ear begins to throb a bit. I think maybe it's the intense stillness that causes it. Perhaps the gun shot was a loud noise that has made my ear sensitive to such quiet moments. I wish this throbbing would go away. It will probably take a few more days, but I want it to heal now. I want to be able to enjoy this moment for a little while longer. Because, right now in this moment, I don't have to do anything, be anyone or figure anything out. But, it won't stop and it's bothersome. It's nagging. And it reminds me of the asshole in a black suit who is responsible for it.

In the background, amidst the sounds of Mother Nature, is the stirring roar of her force. Growing in sound with each footstep, I can tell we are getting closer to the edge of the island. The undeniable commotion of water crashing against the rocks is exciting. I can see up ahead that the brush ends and the view opens up, and so I quicken my pace. Walking to the end of the path and entering into a wide open field my feet slow down. The earth on which we're walking ends about twenty feet up ahead on our right hand side. About a mile, straight ahead in the distance, is the Montauk Lighthouse and we could walk there if we stay along the edge of the cliff and follow it. We creep further south, to our right hand side, and look out onto the Atlantic.

"This is it," I acknowledge. "The end."

"It just stops right here? Just like that?" Joc tip toes closer. I cautiously follow.

We get as close as three inches from the cut-off. Four more inches and our toes would be hanging off the side of Long Island. It's about an eighty foot drop down to the rocks and sand that are constantly battered by the ocean waves.

The bright yellow sun brings out the blue in the ocean and the contrast of the great blue surface and the scattering of pure whitecaps make for the front of a postcard.

"This is the spot," I say.

I don't look over to see if Joe agrees, I just hear him acknowledge my sentiments. "Yep, we're not going to find a better place than this."

I take a deep breath, I haven't smelled the ocean in a while. I smell flowers all day at work, but I haven't been to the beach in two years. The ocean smells… big… and new.

"Should we dig a hole or just open the thing up and let the ashes fly?" Joe asks.

I never thought about it. Joe answers his own question. "I say we dig a hole right here."

That's fine with me. "Okay."

We both take two big rocks that are bigger than our fists and start to frantically scrape away at the dirt. I wait until we dig a hole about five to six inches deep and then I put my rock down and stand up.

I lower one strap of the backpack off my shoulder and swing it around to the front of my abdomen. I get the zipper open all the way, reach in and grab the urn with two hands. This is it. I begin to twist the cap of the urn to open it and eventually get it completely loose. Before I can pull the cap up, a quiet voice interrupts me.

"Even after all this time…"

Joe rises to his feet with his hands up and I spin around with the urn raised. We are ready to defend ourselves but the man who startled us is about ten feet from us. He's softly smiling and gripping a leash that holds a black Labrador on the opposite end of it. His eyes look beyond us.

He continues. "Even after all this time, the sun never says to the earth, 'You owe me.' Look what happens with a love like that, it lights up the whole sky."

"What the hell, man?" Joe blurts out and transitions his hands from the front of his face to his chest.

The old man with wavy platinum hair fixes his glance onto us. "That's one of my favorite quotations from an old Sufi poet who had great insight into the nature of all things." His eyes move back to the scene behind us. "That's quite a symphony, huh? Colors, smells, objects in motion. What an experience."

My heart rate settles, but my mind begins to race.

"What are you doing here?" Joe asks.

The man looks behind him at the dirt path we had just taken ourselves. "I come here all the time. I enjoy the quiet. I enjoy the space between the noise and the vibration of the moment. Walking through this place and taking in this view allows that pesky little idea to come creeping back into the forefront of my mind. That idea that there's more, more to you and me. The story is not a single, tiny frantic chapter but an epic tale that fills billions of pages. This moment of solitude here can help you become aware of that."

I raise my eyebrows, lower the urn and look behind myself. It is pretty incredible I'll give him that. "It's like night and day from the military scene next door."

"Well how would we know silence without clatter? They depend on each other." He looks down at his dog. "Waldo and I enjoy walking through the whole park. Acres and acres of experience. Something new every day."

Out of the corner of my mind I can see the wheels spinning inside Joe's head.

"You named your dog, Waldo?" he finally manages.

"Yes," the man says matter-of-factly.

"Well…" Joe says and looks to me for help, but I don't know how to politely tell someone to piss off. I personally don't mind the man too much, but he did interrupt our ceremony. On the other hand, he's friendly and in this moment of peace I don't want to be the asshole. Joe looks down at my hands which still grip the urn.

The man notices as well. "What brings you guys out here? A man's final wish?"

"Uhhh," is all I can utter as I tighten the cap of the urn.

The man continues, "Is that all he wanted?"

His prying seems invasive and for some reason Joe and I stiffen up in defense.

"We have something to attend to," Joe quickly answers.

"In private," I add.

"A family member?" the man asks.

"Yes, he was." I answer.

The incredible clashing of the ocean waves on the rocks is suddenly and abruptly drowned out by the sound of rubber ripping through gravel. The source can't be seen but it gets louder as it gets closer. I frown at Joe, his eyes widen.

"Cars," he says and then listens... "Multiple cars."

The sound is coming from the north, on the other side of the brush and trees. I quickly begin to put the urn away and zipper the backpack up.

"No!" Joe grabs my hand. "Dump it."

"Now?" I ask.

"Where else are we going to do it?" he asks. "Dump it here."

"Let's go take a look and see who is over there," I say.

The man with the dog tightens his grip on the leash and looks behind him again, back down the path that we've all just walked. "Are you guys expecting someone?" he asks.

"Listen, man," Joe starts, "you might want to get a move on. Take Waldo and keep walking." Then Joe grabs the backpack but I clench my two hands around it. "Jack, just give it to me and I'll do it. You don't have to worry about it anymore. Let me empty it out right here in the hole we've dug."

I don't release my grip. It doesn't feel right. It feels rushed. It feels sloppy. And if I just dump him right here and then run it would feel, I don't know, unfinished.

"We have to go make sure that those cars aren't who we think they are," I tell Joe as I stare into his eyes and don't blink. "That's the priority now."

"You guys are being chased?" the man asks.

Joe steps toward him. "Man, I told you to get out of here." Then Joe moves across the front of me and motions to follow him. Looking back he says, "This is the best place to leave the urn, Jack. It's dead weight now. Just put the whole bag down and let's see what's going on over there." He points beyond the brush.

"Did you tell somebody you were here?" the man wonders.

"Mind your own business," Joe scolds and walks away.

"Your business is my business now," the man replies.

"This is none of your business!" Joe yells.

"Sure it is. You want to know all about him, don't you?"

Joe halts. I turn. The man continues.

"You want to know what all this is about? Well, that *is* my business. I can tell you about it because I'm a part of the story myself. But if you're really being followed then I need to know more and this is not the time nor the place to talk so we have to move away from here."

"Who are you, old man?" Joe asks.

"Just call me... the Sailor," he says.

I approach the man earnestly. "Do you really know why we are here? Honestly? And if you do, start talking."

The Sailor nods his head up and down. "You are here because of a name. And I will tell you about it but not here and not now. First, follow me."

"No," I reply and then take a long, hard swallow before taking one more step towards him. "Tell us the name first." I need validation.

The Sailor quickly glances beyond the brush where the cars are heard swarming and then he comes back and looks me dead in the eyes. "It's Harold Gordon, of course."

Validation complete.

Chapter 7: Get Out

"Now, we should get moving," the Sailor advises.

"Where do we go?" I ask him.

He turns to his left and points in the opposite direction of the path that we entered in on. "There... head along the coastline. About fifty yards down and around the corner there is a path on the left that will funnel you guys into a small clearing. In front of you to the north, there will be a wall of bushes where you will be able to peek through to see into the south parking lot of Camp Hero. Stay low to the ground. If it turns out to be who you fear it is, come back out of the clearing and keep moving east along the coastline until you get to the site of Battery Dunn 216. Once you hit Battery 216, turn and head straight north through the brush. You're going to be running through trees and thorn bushes. Keep pushing through, make sure you're going north the whole time and you will be able to get out of the park's perimeters and run smack dab into a main road. This will be the main road you initially drove in on."

"Where will you be?" I ask.

"I'm going back down this path toward the radar antennae to get my car. I will meet you on that main road and pick you up. Stay low in the brush until you see a red Jeep, that's me."

And with that, Waldo and he begin to walk one way and Joe and I sprint the other. As we run, the urn on my back bounces up and down inside the backpack and our breaths keep pace with each bounce.

Up, down, in, out, up, down, in, out. Our feet stomping accordingly, as well.

When I look over my shoulder the Sailor is still visible but getting smaller and smaller. I can barely make out his figure but can see that he's holding Waldo's leash in his left hand and holding something up to his ear with his right. A phone, perhaps.

"Can we trust this guy?" Joe manages while still running.

"I don't know."

"If anything happens, he's too old to overpower us." Joe's already planning his defense.

We round the corner and follow the path to the left.

"This running sucks," Joe says in between gasps.

"I know." … *Captain Obvious*.

We get to the small clearing that allows us to look through the wall of bushes inconspicuously and see the south parking lot of Camp Hero.

Nothing. No familiar cars. One motorcycle, parked, but that's it.

"I heard more than one motorcycle," Joe says.

"Me too."

"Maybe what we heard wasn't them, though," Joe reasons.

"Maybe," I echo. "So should we meet up with the Sailor?"

"If nobody's chasing us then I say we just find our driver and have him take us back to the Manor."

"But *somebody's* here, we heard it."

"Well, they're not here right now," Joe notes and turns.

He begins to walk away. My thoughts turn toward figuring a way out of Camp Hero. *Should we follow the Sailor's instructions or should we find our car and driver?* It's an honest debate that I begin to give attention to until we hear it again; rubber ripping through gravel. We duck our heads and return to the wall of bushes just in time to see two SUV's come ripping into the lot. Their tires are skidding and fast-paced. One SUV takes the top half of the parking lot and one takes the bottom half. They constantly circle their halves. I can see faces pressed against the glass inside the car, searching the brush as they turn. Joe and I get lower to the ground until they appear to be satisfied and head back out of the parking lot.

How'd they find us?

"Now, we go," Joe directs.

We run back down the path until we reach the intersecting coastline. I look to the west and can make out the Sailor coming toward us in the distance but this time, Waldo is not with him.

I double-take and look again. *That's not the Sailor.* It's someone running after us and they're gaining ground.

"Joe," I point. "Run!"

And with that I take off and pull ahead of Joe. He, of course, looks behind himself, yells out, 'ah shit!' and rivals me for first place. It's a mini-race between us. He pulls ahead and then I pick up the pace. There's a constant back and forth that keeps us running at an above-average speed.

Now, the synchronizing beats of our feet, our breaths, and the bouncing of the urn pick up to a 'presto' tempo. My ear throbs from the over-activity and raised blood pressure.

I swallow. My mouth's losing saliva. Swallowing is becoming a difficult task.

I glance back again only to see that we haven't made any progress in escaping and that the person is actually, now, about twenty yards away. Except, this person isn't wearing a black suit and tie like the others. This person is wearing a black windbreaker with a neon green-colored trim. I slow down as I focus on getting a better look.

"Pick it up, Jack!" Joe yells back.

This person is wearing headphones. This person is sporting white running shoes. This person is not chasing us, they're just running. When they get ten yards away I stop completely.

"Jack, what are you doing?!" Joe looks back to see the same thing I do. He stops running as well as the runner passes by us with an absolute look of confusion and fear on their face.

Joe exhales. "You gotta be kidding me." He leans over and grabs his knees with his hands; resting his entire body upon his legs.

I look up to the sky and throw my hands on top of my head.

"That was messed up," Joe complains.

"It's better than the alternative," I note.

We try to catch our breaths. It doesn't work very well.

"Let's keep moving, Joe."

We walk along.

"I see something up ahead," Joe says.

I look for myself and see it too: a giant concrete slab in the dirt with a sign next to it. This is where Battery Dunn 216 used to be. We approach the site and position ourselves north.

"Straight through that brush and we'll hit the main road," I say.

"Are we sure we want to go this way?" he asks.

"We can't go back the same way we came in. Our only way is forward."

Joe sighs and slowly starts to enter the brush. He pushes and pulls away branches that are in front of him. I look back to check our tail and hope that nobody is noticing us. I catch something in my glance. It's too far away down the coastline to make out; it's just two moving blobs in the distance. I cover my body by stepping into the brush but stick my head out to continue my observation. The blobs with their soft, unspecific edges slowly begin to take shape and the corners of their being become distinct with each footstep forward. Their black attire becomes clearer and more evident. They're not running, just walking, looking around. They don't see me. Joe is about fifteen steps deep into the brush already. I quickly follow him.

"Joe, we have to hurry through this. They're coming down the coastline, scanning the area."

The cracking of twigs and rustling of leaves beneath each step we take is the only evidence as to our whereabouts. Everything else- the smacking of branches into our face and the thorns scraping across our arms and legs, we suffer from quietly. We curse the brush with muffled caveman-like grunts. After about one hundred yards we stop completely and listen for nearby cars or trailing footsteps behind us. Silence. Our ears are our biggest ally right now as the brush completely covers our view around us. We are hidden, yet blind.

We continue through the thicket and as we do, an image enters my mind: the Sailor on his phone. *And now there are men walking in from the same direction that I saw him walking toward when we split up. Did he send them after us by pointing them in our direction? Or are we being sent straight into their arms? Our other option, the alternative, is to stop walking completely and just hide here. Hide and hope they don't find us.*

It's sort of as if we've exited a dark movie theater and stumbled outside into pure sunlight. One second we're crunching twigs and leaves beneath our feet and the next step we're on dirt soil, and the heavy branches that we've been swatting away from our faces are now replaced with a refreshing breeze and a view of the main road.

I grab Joe's shoulder. "Stay back in here for a moment and don't let anybody see you."

We seep backward into obscurity.

We hear the running motor of a car slowly approaching so we crouch down.

"Make sure nobody else is in the car with him," I whisper.

A red Jeep cruises in front of us, flashes its lights and slows down to a crawl. We stand up to walk out but another car motor is heard coming from behind the Sailor's Jeep. We fall back down to our bellies and hide. A black SUV pulls up alongside the Jeep and rolls down its window. I hold my breath so I can hear what's being said.

"Whatcha doing out here, old timer?" the man in the passenger seat of the black SUV asks.

"Just getting ready to head back home after a walk through the park with my dog," the Sailor answers and rustles Waldo's fur.

"Why are you driving so slow along the side of the road?" the man asks.

"Ah," the Sailor acts aggravated. "My dog was jumping back and forth from the passenger seat to the

151

back seat and I had to settle him down. I didn't want to get into an accident so I pulled off a bit."

"I see," the man says. "You were walking your dog inside Camp Hero State Park?" the man asks.

"Yes."

"Did you see anybody else walking around in there? Anybody that was inside the camp site?"

"No, no I don't believe I did, sir," the Sailor says.

"Alright, be careful driving with that dog," the man finishes and then rolls up the window as the SUV speeds off.

We wait a second. The red Jeep slowly creeps along until the SUV is out of site and then the Jeep stops completely on the side of the road.

Joe turns to me, "Let's go."

We catch up to the car. I knock on the passenger side window and the Sailor waves us in.

"We're going to have to be fast, they're all around this area. Keep your heads down," the Sailor advises.

I slouch down into my seat and fold my knees up so that my shins rest against the front of the glove compartment. Joe closes the back door and leans forward; Waldo sits to his left.

"What is it about Harold Gordon that's making them come after us? We don't know him, we never met him and we've never heard of him," I ask.

"It's not you that they're after," the Sailor says.

"Then what did Harold Gordon do that's making him such a wanted man?"

"You really don't know what's going on?" he inquires.

"No!" Joe screams from the backseat.

"Harold Gordon is not in the present tense anymore," the Sailor informs.

The Sailor checks his watch and looks forward like he's giving the SUV time to get a good lead ahead of us so we don't run into them again.

"You mean he's dead?" I ask.

"Yes."

The Sailor punches the Jeep forward.

"Then what did he do when he was alive?" I want to know.

"He didn't do anything."

The Sailor merges back onto the main road and keeps up the pace.

"Then why all this fuss over a dead man who didn't do anything?" I wonder.

"It's not Harold Gordon they're after."

"Who, then?"

"They're after the people that killed him." The Sailor responds.

Chapter 8: Run Away

My mind goes blank for a moment. I can't think straight, there's no clarity.

Joe, with his never-ending ability to find just the right words at such moments as this breaks the deafening silence. "What the shit does that mean?!" he blurts out.

If I string all of this information together I might be able to understand what the Sailor is trying to say, but I can't bring myself to do it right now. Literally, I need more than a moment to organize my thoughts.

The Sailor slows the Jeep down a bit. "In order for this conversation to continue, I need to know exactly what your father told you before he died."

"How did you know about our father?" I ask.

"My brother and I knew your father well," the Sailor says.

"Your brother?"

"You met him not long ago at the golf course. He called me after you guys left and said that he sent you to

Camp Hero. He said Carl Miller told you about Harold Gordon."

"Carl Miller didn't tell us shit about Harold Gordon!" Joe counters. "He's merely haunting us with his name. Dropping it here and there and inciting people to chase us at the mere mention of it."

"Yes, well," the Sailor starts, "when my brother said that you guys were coming here I told him I would come and see what it was that you knew and it appears that you're going at this thing blind."

"That's accurate," I say.

"But your father is Carl Miller and he wants you to know about Harold Gordon, right?" he asks.

"My father sent a bouquet of flowers, posthumously, to a doctor's office in Holtsville. Harold Gordon was the name on the delivery tag. Shortly after I attempted to deliver the bouquet of flowers all hell broke loose and that's how this all started," I explain to him.

The car slows down as the Sailor presses on the brake and spins his neck ninety-degrees to look at me. "Say that again," he instructs.

Just then a honking is heard from behind. I look in the rearview mirror to see a white pick-up truck quickly approaching.

The Sailor tilts his head to the left and slightly leans his body out the window to use the driver side mirror. "What does *he* want now?"

The honking grows louder as the pick-up truck swerves to the left to avoid crashing into our tailgate. The truck pulls up alongside us; it's the Starter. He rolls down his passenger side window.

"What the hell are you doing?!" the Starter screams at his brother.

"I was going to ask you the same thing!" our driver yells back.

"You're not helping them, are you?!"

The Sailor doesn't answer the question.

"Don't be stupid! I sent the cops to Camp Hero to find those two!" the Starter exclaims.

"You're the reason those men showed up?!" the Sailor yells.

"Yes! Now pull over!"

The white pick-up inches closer to the Jeep and the Sailor gives the wheel a tug to the right and slams on the brakes, bringing his car to a halt on a dirt patch on the side of the road.

The white pick-up skids about fifteen feet in front of us and comes to a stop as well. A fog of dirt fills the air as the Starter gets out of his car and the Sailor opens up his door. I put my right hand on the handle with the intent to follow.

"Stay here a moment, let me talk to him," the Sailor instructs and continues out of his vehicle and cuts his brother off at the front hood of the Jeep, leaving his door open.

"You shouldn't be driving like that, Earl. You could've cause an accident," the Sailor scolds.

The Starter pulls out his phone. "Those two are supposed to be in custody right now."

"I don't think you understand," the Sailor puts his hand on top of his brother's phone to deny him from dialing.

"Oh, I understand perfectly," the Starter says, "Carl is trying to sell us down the river, trying to blow the lid on us." His voice lowers, "I don't care if he *is* dead, he has them trying to find out what happened. We need to nip this in the bud right now, brother."

"Earl, maybe it's time," the Sailor says.

"No, no," his brother waves his finger, steps back and bends over as a coughing fit begins.

The Sailor steps forward to comfort him. "Carl reached out to his kids, he wants them to know the truth."

"No!" the Starter shouts in between coughs and covers his mouth with his hand until he is able to settle down, catch his breath and finally swallow. "Can't you see what's happening? Can't you see what Carl is doing?"

"What?" the Sailor asks.

"I bet you it was him. Maybe we were wrong the first time, but not this time. I bet you *he* was the one. And with those boys out there sniffing around, we're in danger. Carl wants to confess *and* implicate us? That's too bad, he can't do that. I won't allow it. I won't let him take me down with him." He raises his phone again, and again the Sailor pushes it down.

"Are you crazy?!" the Starter emphatically asks. "Stop it right now." He moves to use the phone again but the sound of a vehicle's engine gets everybody's attention. The two brothers turn to see what's coming. I look out the back window of the Jeep to see it too: a black Crown Victoria.

The Starter runs out into the middle of the road with his hands up in the air. "Stop! Stop!" he yells, but it's quickly cut short by another fit of coughs.

"Earl! Put your hands down!" the Sailor demands. Then he turns to us and gets back into the car, throws the

Jeep in drive and spins out until finally settling the car back onto the concrete road.

Joe and I look back to see the Crown Vic halt for the Starter in the middle of the road. We can see him run around to the driver's side, point toward us and then step away as the Crown Vic begins to pursue us.

"They're coming," I warn.

The Sailor puts more pressure on the gas and the Jeep lunges forward. The vibration from the steering wheel shakes the excess skin on the old man's arms but the focus in his eyes is unwavering.

"What was your brother talking about?" Joe asks from the back.

"I have a slip at Montauk Marina," the Sailor says, "I made a phone call right after we split up on the bluffs. If we can make it to the docks there's a boat waiting for us," he explains.

That must've been the phone call I saw him make… *But we barely talked to him before that.*

"You arranged a boat after only meeting us for one minute?" I ask out loud.

"You want to know why you're in Montauk, right?"

"Of course," I answer.

"I need time to tell you," he explains.

Joe leans forward. "So you want to take us out into a boat and tell us? No, no, no, tell us right now," he demands.

"We're pre-occupied right now," the Sailor counters.

I look behind us to see what he's talking about; our pursuers are about forty yards away.

"No!" Joe yells. "You and your brother are hiding something and you want us to go for a boat ride with you? I don't even want to be in this car with you. Matter of fact, pull over right now!"

Joe's got a point about the discussion the two brothers just had.

"What *were* you and your brother talking about?" I ask him.

"Before you do anything else, you're telling us what that was all about," Joe adds.

The Sailor's eyes maintain focus on the road.

"You said Harold Gordon was murdered, right?" I instigate.

A moment. The Sailor's bony fingers re-grip the steering wheel. "Yes, he was," the Sailor answers.

"Why was he murdered?" I ask.

He checks the rearview mirror first before he answers. "Because he was thought to be a spy for the Soviet Union."

Thought to be?

"Was he a really a Soviet spy?" I pry.

"Some time after his death it was concluded that he, most likely, was not." The Sailor shifts his hands to the 10 and 2 position.

"So he was murdered for no reason?" I ask.

"Even the senseless makes sense when you peel back the layers." He glances over at his driver side mirror. I check mine as well; they're gaining more ground on us.

The Sailor continues. "There was heavy suspicion of a Soviet spy inside the Montauk Air Force base at Camp Hero. He was thought to be gathering intelligence on the new radar being built for the Semi-Automatic Ground Environment system."

"And was there? Was there really a spy?"

"Classified papers were thought to be compromised and classified blueprints for the S.A.G.E. radar were reported to have gone missing from the base and then re-appeared days later."

"Did they ever find out what was happening or who it was?" I probe.

"No," he says.

"But Harold Gordon was fingered for it?"

"Yes."

"By who?" Joe joins in.

"By a group of his peers," he replies.

"And they killed him?" I ask.

"Yes," he responds quickly.

The black car behind us is now less than thirty yards away and still coming strong. We won't be able to out run them.

I take a moment before I ask the Sailor my next question. I fear the answer.

"Sir," I preface. "Who exactly killed Harold Gordon?"

The Sailor's hands don't move or shift positions on the steering wheel. He is still and calm. "We all did," he admits.

I swallow. "My father?"

"Yes… and my brother, myself and a fella by the name of Tom Lansky."

The car loses all oxygen and again, I lose focus on my thoughts. All at once they spring around inside my head with no clear intent other than to cause dizziness.

Joe is heard shifting his weight in the backseat. "You've got to be kidding me," he declares.

"It's not a joke," the Sailor retorts. "Out of suspicion, we accused Harold Gordon of being a spy. Because of fear, we killed him."

Chapter 9: Fight Back

I try to connect the dots before I can even process the information. It's like running with a dead leg. I have an idea of where I want to go with my next question but it just takes a moment until I can finally get there.

"Who else knows about the killing of Harold Gordon?"

"Before today, the four of us never said a word to anyone else. Your father has broken that silence."

"A final confession from a man on his deathbed," Joe says. "I guess he didn't have time to tell us all of his regrets so he just picked the biggest one," he jokes.

"These men behind us, how'd they find out about all of this?" I ask.

"I'm not certain," the Sailor replies.

"But wait," Joe starts and then stops and thinks before continuing. "If they're after the people that killed Harold Gordon then what do we have to worry for, Jack? Why are we still running? We didn't do anything."

"We still have to get on that boat," the Sailor says.

"What? No we don't. You already told us what the hell is going on. Come to think about it, all we have to do is turn you and your brother over to the authorities. You're the guilty party, you're who they are ultimately after. This is open and shut as far as I'm concerned." Joe swipes his hands together several times to signify the end of his physical and mental participation in this investigation.

"I want to know how it happened," I impulsively state out loud. It was true, I want more. Honestly, I'm still wary of believing it all. I know Carl Miller was not close to perfect but this? If this is true then this old man is going to have to prove it.

"So you want the details?" Joe sounds disgusted.

"I want more information." I need to continue to process my active and unruly thoughts.

Joe speaks up again. "Well, I don't need to continue on this wild goose chase anymore. I don't need to run from the law and I sure as hell don't want to die in this high-speed chase sitting next to Waldo the fucking dog!" Joe emphatically points to the innocent pooch. "I want off this ride. I don't care about this anymore and come to think of it, I never did."

I object to my brother's claim. "Of course you cared or else you wouldn't have come in the first place."

"Do you have selective memory?" He leans forward and pours on the patronizing tone. "I was talked into this silly adventure by you and my gullible wife. She seemed to think Carl was a good guy and you seemed to think this little road trip would solve everything."

I immediately feel the urge to defend myself. My heart races and my chest tightens. "We both wanted answers to the questions that we've had for so many years! Are you too arrogant to admit that?"

"The only thing I'll admit is that my wife and I haven't been getting along well lately and I needed to get out of the house for a day or two so, I did. But this? If I had known it was going to be like this..." He obnoxiously laughs.

"Nobody knew it was going to be like this, Joe."

"Then why don't you just agree with me? We've seen enough. Surprise! All this time we thought he was just a bad father, but it turns out he was an even shittier human being!"

His words burn the pit of my gut.

"Now pull this car over and let me out," Joe demands.

I don't know what to do. I imagine, for a moment, pulling over and ending this all. Giving up right here. It feels... incomplete and hollow.

I turn to the Sailor, "Can you tell us more?"

He takes his eyes off the road to look at me. "I'll tell you everything I know."

"Did you hear what I said?" Joe leans forward and sticks his head in between the two front seats. "Let me out of this car right now, old man."

"Sit back and put your seat belt on," the Sailor responds, "both of you." He tightens his grip on the steering wheel. I notice the black blur out of the corner of my eye. They've caught up and they're hovering behind our tailgate.

Joe doesn't obey. "You're not listening to what I said. Turn your hearing aid up. Slow down, pull over and let me out. I don't want to participate anymore." Then he looks down at the floor between my feet. "And get rid of this thing already!" He lunges forward and grabs the backpack and pulls it toward himself. I grab onto it before he can totally get full possession.

"What are you doing? Stop!" I instruct him.

"I'm putting an end to this. He said he wanted to be buried in Montauk, right? Well he wasn't specific on a location so, I'm taking creative liberties. I'm going to bury him right outside this car." He starts rolling down his window.

"No!" I yell. Waldo barks. My right hand reaches over and grabs the top of the backpack and with a ferocious pull, the urn-filled backpack flies back into my possession. The sudden tug and my vocal outburst freezes Joe for a moment. Then he sighs and leans back.

"Jack," he throws his hands up and then allows them to come down and slap against his lap. "I'm sorry you needed this, I really am. But I have a life. I don't need any more answers than I already have gotten. I'm content."

The Crown Vic sways back and forth behind us.

"If you're content then why do you still carry the anger?" the Sailor asks.

Joe points his finger into the side of the man's face and brings back that condescending tone. "Didn't I tell you to do something with this car?"

Joe was right about me. I don't have a life like he does. I don't have the marriage and the nice house and a well-paying job. I don't wear suits to work or drive a car that turns heads. I know that I'm not successful. I don't do anything special. My life doesn't serve any great purpose other than to pay rent and taxes. I allow others to live well with my financial contributions. That's all that

I've done. That's it. It's true. The river is deep and the current is strong and it's exhausting work staying afloat. But, dad reached out with a branch and I grabbed on. That branch was a note attached to flowers.

I search my pockets for it but of course it's not there. I left it in my old pair of pants so I close my eyes to picture it in my mind: *You cannot stop until you find out the truth and experience it for yourself. Then, I hope, you will take the most significant action. Then I hope you will do the one thing I couldn't do.*

Was the truth he was referring to the truth about what he did to Harold Gordon? I can't be certain because then he goes on: *Then I hope you will do the one thing I couldn't do.* But what is that one thing?

I conclude: *I'm not letting go of this branch.*

The Crown Vic tries to pull up along our right side but the Sailor quickly changes lanes to cut it off and it settles back behind us again, waiting for its next move. I look up ahead and see flashing lights. There's a black SUV parked across the middle of the road trying to block both lanes. There's driving room to the right of the road. It's about twenty feet of dirt and then further to the right of that is forest. To the left side of the road there's a natural median comprised of bushes and a few skinny trees mixed in. It separates the road we are currently on, which is heading west, from the road that heads back east toward the end of the island.

The Jeep slows down. "It's about time you finally came to your senses," Joe says.

We're now one hundred yards away from crashing into the SUV ahead. The Crown Vic pulls up alongside my door to make sure we can't veer off the road to the right and go around the SUV. I'm no more than six feet away from the man behind the wheel, with our faces separated only by two panes of glass. I can see the outline of the driver's face, the details of it stay hidden in the dark because of their heavily- tinted windows. My face, however, is exposed as the frames of his shades turn and point right at me.

We are fifty yards away and the Sailor still has us doing about 50 m.p.h.

"Slow down!" Joe grips the back of my seat.

"Hold on!" the Sailor replies and with that he yanks the wheel to the left.

The Crown Victoria races passed us. I put my right elbow up to stop my head from slamming into the passenger window. Waldo ends up in Joe's lap and I can see the Sailor struggling to control the wheel as the vehicle bursts through a wall of bushes. I grab to help the old man steer us across the forest-like median to avoid clipping any trees. We end up coasting into the middle of the road on the other side. Instead of turning left to head east the Sailor cuts the wheel right to go against the traffic. The glare of the sun beams off the hood of a small sedan that's coming right at us. The steering wheel bounces left to avoid a collision and veers off down a small dirt driveway. A quick glance backwards reveals no black vehicles in tow. Through the scattered trees, a small yellow house can be seen with a barn-like shed beside it. The Jeep bounces along with each hole its tires hit.

"Holy shit," Joe can be heard saying, followed by the sound of his back door opening. By the time I look he's already leaning outside. "Stop the car!"

This time, the Sailor complies. The Jeep stops right in front of the small house at the pinnacle of its horse-shoe shaped dirt driveway.

"Where are you going to go?" I ask as I open my door as well.

"Home," Joe slams the door behind him.

"How?"

"I'll figure it out, Jack. Maybe these people will let me borrow their car," he says sarcastically. "If they're home."

"They are," the Sailor answers and opens the back door for Waldo to hop out.

"How do you know?" I wonder.

"Because this is where I live," he responds. "We're going to switch cars right now and head to the docks."

He heads to the front door of his house and lets Waldo inside then shuts the door again.

"I'll hitchhike," Joe says.

The Sailor walks into the shed.

"Joe, if they catch you-"

"They're not going to hurt us, Jack." He starts walking down the right side of the driveway.

A car engine roars from inside the shed.

"Joe, couldn't you just stick around for a little longer?" I follow after him.

"For what?!" He laughs maniacally. "No. I'm done!"

He continues to walk away from me. I stop and stare at his back. With the incredible firepower that it holds, my mind, in no more than three seconds, imagines the rest of my entire life: its mundanity, its fleetingness, its irrelevance. In the far corner of my mind, it imagines it all without my brother and I wonder if I'll ever see him again.

"Joe!" I call to the back of his head and utter the first words that come to mind, which happen to be the most honest words in my heart. "I want you to stay!"

That takes a lot for me to do. It's merely five words but inside of them holds a lifetime of truth and honesty. My feelings about my brother have finally been verbalized in a single act of desperation. I don't believe that I ever truly hated my brother. Avoided him? Yes. Annoyed by him? At times. But truly hated him? I can't say that I ever did. Then what happened to us? To our brotherhood? *Was it ever there?*

And now, I want to continue to be honest with him. "Why haven't we stayed in touch?"

Joe turns his body and faces me. He starts to shake his head little by little. He sighs and shrugs his shoulders. Anything besides words.

I go on, "All these years and it's dad that gets us back together."

Joe searches the ground for a verbal response. "That son of a bitch let us down, time and time again. He doesn't deserve all of this attention."

"I don't believe the Sailor, Joe. He's going to have to prove that what he's saying is true."

Joe looks up and to the left. "I just want to go back to two days ago before any of this even existed."

"You mean without me?" I ask.

"I didn't say that," Joe insists. "He just- he mistreated us, Jack. Why treat him any differently than the way he did us? Everything he did was like he thought, in the back of his mind, that his whole life would've been far greater had we never been a part of it."

The moments that Joe is alluding to, the moments that dad betrayed us, pierce me. "Why didn't we ever stick up for each other, Joe?"

Joe sniffs and throws up his hands. He doesn't acknowledge the question. "This whole time, we're supposed to be burying him, not digging him up." He hesitates then says, "I just want to forget him."

"But you never will," I remind.

He's about to say more but stops, turns and continues down the path toward the main road. Away from me.

Tires roll up behind me and when I turn around there's a Honda Civic waiting so, I open the passenger door and sit down. I comb my hair with my hand and kick my legs out. I have leg space. *Why?*

"Hold on," I instruct the Sailor and then hop out and jog over to the Jeep and pull the handle. It's locked. "Open the Jeep!" I call to him. He rolls down his window and throws me the key. I slide it in, open the door and grab the backpack off the floor.

"Leave the key in the cup holder!" the Sailor calls out.

I comply, then shut the door and jog back around to the Honda and right before I jump in again I see a motionless figure out of the corner of my eye. It's Joe and he's stopped walking. He briefly looks at me before turning back away. I sink into the Civic and close the door. The Sailor takes off down the left side of the horse-shoe driveway. It doesn't immediately lead straight to the main road but narrows a bit to the left. It's longer than the right-sided path we entered on and more enclosed. Woods surround it on both sides and it's just wide enough for one vehicle. The 'light at the end of the tunnel' can be seen up ahead. It's a small opening of sunlight that shines onto the concrete road. Our vision of the road is only as wide as that opening. We have to approach it cautiously. We creep the nose of the Civic out into the sunlight and peak our heads forward to try and look to the right for on-coming traffic. The black SUV is ten yards to our right and passing by our nose. The Sailor doesn't panic, he just clears his throat. The driver of the black SUV presses his forehead against the window and I feel exposed again and he inspects our car. *Please don't stop, please don't stop.* The SUV drives by and I exhale. Then it slams on its brakes and spins its tires in reverse.

Oh Shit.

The Sailor doesn't waste any time as he throws the car into reverse and slams on the gas. I look back at the trail. It's so narrow. The Sailor puts his right hand onto the back of my seat to help his head turn further backward. I face forward again. The SUV is already facing us with its headlights chasing after ours. The Sailor begins to breathe heavy. The car shifts quickly, left to right, as he tries to keep us on the path. The SUV increases speed and lunges forward toward the hood of the Civic, crashing down on top of it, effectively pinning our front tires against the ground. The frantic footwork of the Sailor to accelerate his smaller car out of the clasp of the SUV makes for little progress and proves futile. Just to make sure of it, the man in the passenger seat hangs out of the window brandishing a gun and fires three rounds into our front left tire. Both vehicles stop and two men in black suits immediately hop out of the SUV and point their weapons at us.

"Out of the vehicle with your hands up!" one man yells.

I sit frozen. The Sailor slowly puts his hands up. We wait until the two men each take a side and open our respective doors. I try not to make eye contact with the black firearm. I'm aware of my ear again. *Was this the bastard who rang my eardrum?* On cue, it throbs again.

"Get up and get out!" the man yells and then grabs me by my shirt and rips me from the seat.

He looks my face over, pointing a familiar pair of sunglasses my way. "Different car, same face," he says. Then he smirks and throws my chest against the side of the car and pats me down with one hand while his other hand, with the gun, ensures I don't make any sudden movements. I look across the hood and see the Sailor staring back at me.

"Who do you work for?" the Sailor asks.

"Keep your mouth closed," his man responds and whips out a pair of handcuffs. They walk me and the Sailor toward the front of their SUV.

"Tell us where Carl Miller is," the man in my ear demands.

"He's dead," I respond.

"Do you understand what will happen if you lie to us?" the man asks.

"I'm not lying. His ashes are right there on the floor of the passenger seat, inside the backpack."

"Cuff him," the other man says.

"No wait, I'm serious! Just look in the backpack!" I plead.

Cuffs are snapped onto the Sailor and he's walked to the rear side door of the SUV.

"What are we being arrested for?" the Sailor asks.

"Aiding and abetting," the man replies.

The guy in charge of me turns me around to face the SUV. His back is turned to the still-open passenger side door of the Honda Civic. It's about two feet from his back. At the same time that I feel the cold steel of the handcuffs begin to touch my skin, I can hear the roar of a third car. I swing around just in time to see the Sailor's Jeep almost at the tailgate of the Civic. And it's not slowing down. The man holding me turns around to see it as well only he's too late. I jump off to the side of the trail into a blanket of leaves. The Jeep rams the back of the Civic and folds it up against the front of the black SUV like an accordion. Everything shifts at least ten feet forward, including the still-open passenger door which slams into the man in the black suit and sends him flying towards the front of the SUV and bouncing off its driver side mirror.

I roll over and see the carnage of the Jeep tucked up under the back of the Civic and then roll back to see the man on the floor, motionless. On the other side of the SUV the Sailor's man is walking towards the Jeep with his gun drawn.

"Out of the car, now!"

I rise to my knees and feel my hands touch the ground in front of me.

My hands are free?

He never got the cuffs on me in time.

The door of the Jeep opens and out steps my brother, Joe. The gun gets put in his face while his right hand is grabbed and he's pulled down to the ground.

"Kiss the ground!" the man yells, but Joe doesn't take the instruction well. From his knees, he turns and grabs the gun with both hands. The man holds on and goes for a ride as Joe rises and uses his leverage to pull and flip the man over his back. The man begins to punch Joe in the face with his free hand, but Joe doesn't let go. I hurry to my feet and climb over the top of the disheveled Honda Civic. When I get to the scrum I grab the man's free hand, place my knee on top of his wrist and tell Joe to 'free the gun.' Using both hands, he pries the weapon from the man's intense grip and takes no time in pointing the barrel of the gun at the man on the floor.

"You're making a mistake," the man says as he fans out all ten of his fingers on both hands and shows Joe his palms. "Don't do anything foolish."

Joe keeps the gun aimed at the man. I notice the Sailor with his hands behind his back.

"Give us the keys to the handcuffs," I demand.

He slowly moves one hand to his belt and unclips the keys and tosses them to me. The Sailor turns his back to me and I free his hands. He rubs his wrists.

The man on the ground speaks up, "Listen, if you turn yourselves in then we can make sure you don't spend the rest of your life behind bars."

"Lay down, face first," I force the man onto his belly and fasten the cuffs onto him.

"The tires on the SUV are still inflated," the Sailor notices and opens the side door of the black vehicle.

"If you have any morals left in your body or a fraction of a sense of duty to your country, you'd rethink this!" the man yells.

"Stop following us and tell the rest of them to stop as well. We are not trying to hurt anyone," I tell him.

"You're assisting a fugitive," he says. "Carl Miller is-"

"*Was*," I correct him, "Carl Miller *was*." I run to the Civic to prove my point. I grab the backpack, reach in and hold up the urn. "You see, he died the other day. He was our father and now, he's dead. So you can stop following us because we are not helping him hide from anything."

"He's the one you want to talk to," Joe says and points to the Sailor.

"Carl Miller was your father?" the man on the floor asks.

"Yes," I answer and put the urn back in the bag.

"Then we *really* need to question you," the man insists. His voice seems desperate and he looks the part as well with the way he struggles to roll onto his back to make eye contact with us.

"We hardly know anything about what he did," Joe chimes in.

"You may know something that will help us," the man insists.

"Help you do what? Arrest a dead man?" I ask.

"We need to look through his correspondences and all his forms of communication. You may be able to help give us an idea on how long he was active."

I wonder aloud, "Active? In the Air Force?" I turn to the Sailor. "How many years did he serve?"

"No," the man interrupts. "We want to know how long he was an active agent for the Soviet Union."

Chapter 10: The Harold Gordon Story

Through the trees, I can only make out a blurry, black apparition heading up the path towards us. Joe follows my eyes and without saying a word he grabs my arm and runs to the SUV. The Sailor is already in the back seat when I slam the passenger door and throw the backpack onto my lap. The SUV's front bumper is crushed, but Joe is still able to reverse the vehicle and navigate down the dirt path. The folded and damaged Honda Civic and Jeep set a perfect pick between us and the approaching black vehicle.

Upon entering into the sunlight and touching the main road, Joe wastes no time in pivoting and pointing the SUV in the direction of the normal flow of traffic and accelerating.

"Cross the divider again, up ahead, and I'll tell you how to get to Montauk Marina," the Sailor says.

Joe makes a left exactly where the Sailor had crossed the natural median not long ago in a different vehicle. We emerge from our illegal U-turn and head west now. There's no road block this time, they've moved.

"Drive for a mile and then make a right when I tell you," the Sailor instructs.

Nobody else talks. I turn to my left and look at Joe's profile. I know he can see me looking at him but he keeps his eyes on the road.

"You came back," I whisper.

"I saw the first SUV roll past the driveway and then heard it screech its tires on the pavement. I knew that they had spotted you," he says.

"You came back to help us?" I ask him.

A beat of silence.

"I heard gun shots, too," he adds.

"You were worried?" I ask.

Joe picks at the steering wheel with his finger nails.

"You know," he starts, and then licks his lips and scratches his eyebrow.

"What?" I wonder.

"You know, today I received confirmation on something that I've suspected for a long time."

"What's that?" I invite.

"That it's a sad day when your idols let you down. I guess I just figured you've had enough people disappoint you for one lifetime. I didn't want to be another one."

Then he glances at me and smirks and with that, my mind falls back onto the atomic bomb that was Carl Miller's secret occupation.

I look into the back seat. "What was that guy talking about? Why would he say dad was a spy for the Soviet Union?"

The Sailor stares at me for a moment before replying. "I told you there was a suspected spy stealing information."

"You said it was Harold Gordon."

"I said, we thought it was Harold Gordon." The Sailor points passed the windshield. "Turn right up here."

Joe pulls the wheel to the right and masts dressed with sails appear in the distance through the tree tops.

I'm compelled to check the road behind us. I see nothing. But I keep staring. Waiting. Then sure enough, like a black cloud of dust, a black Crown Victoria appears in the distance with another black SUV right behind it.

"We got company again," I tell my fellow travelers.

"No surprise there," I hear the Sailor mutter as Joe looks in the rearview. "Take this road to the end, the Marina entrance is on the right." He then produces his cell phone from his pocket and dials. A moment later he speaks into it. "Hello, Block Island is a green light. I'm going to need you there... Okay, thank you again, we'll see you in a bit."

"Who's that?" I ask.

"That's our getaway plan."

"Where's the entrance?" Joe asks.

"About ten seconds away. When you turn into it, head straight toward the water, stop the car right before the docks and let's get ready to move aboard the boat. The young man who works here should have already gotten it ready to set sail so as soon as we step foot aboard we can motor out. I trust him enough, he's a young, competent kid who works hard."

Joe makes the right into the entrance and rides the car straight toward the water. I grab the backpack and prepare myself to run aboard the awaiting ship. As Joe presses down on the brake pedal I'm already pulling up on the door handle. We hop out and the Sailor points toward the boat that's going to take us to our next destination. It's about twenty feet long with a blue trimming around the top of its otherwise all-white exterior. The words, "S.S. Alan Watts" decorate the side. A young man begins to unlatch one of the two ropes that are keeping the boat docked. The skidding of our pursuer's tires on the pavement behind us causes me to briefly turn around. Four men jump out and run after us. My feet stop hitting against concrete and switch to hitting wooden planks for a short while before ultimately hitting fiberglass and landing safely into the confines of the getaway boat. I swing the backpack over my two shoulders to free my hands and reach out to guide my brother into the boat and then anxiously watch as the old Sailor tries his best to move his experienced body as fast as he can.

The Sailor hits the wooden planks and yells, "Take the last rope off!"

The young man completely unhooks us and the boat begins to glide away from the wooden dock. There's one black-suited man who was clearly at the top of his class during the physical fitness test in training camp. It only takes him about five seconds after the Sailor to hit the wooden planks himself. When the old man is ten feet away from us I reach out my hand and he takes it and lands inside the boat. He staggers to the wheel and pushes the throttle forward sending our entire bodies backwards. I fall and hit my rib cage against the side of the boat. Out of the corner of my eye I can see the black suit leap off the wooden planks across a gap of water and land right behind me. My neck pulls backwards as he grabs hold of the top of my backpack. He's now hanging off the side of the fast-moving boat. From the waist down his body is submerged in salt water and the only thing keeping him from completely falling in is his grip on the bag I have strapped across my back.

I grunt as I become pinned back by his grip and momentum. Joe re-establishes his balance on the boat and notices me.

"Take the bag off!" he yells.

I use all my effort to lean forward, feeling the entire weight of the man's body coming forward as well.

Joe hurries toward me. "Don't pull him into the boat! Slip your shoulders out of the straps!"

I think about what he says, but I refuse. Yes, the man will be released and fall into the water, but so will the bag and the urn that's in it.

"Let it go!" Joe yells at me and tries to pull the straps off my arms.

"No!" I yell back.

My head leans back from the weight being too much to uphold. I can see Joe raise his arms like a gorilla ready to pound its fists against its prey. The rage is back and about to be unleashed.

With each syllable he yells, there is a fist flying downward to accentuate it. "Some. Body. Better. Let. Go. Of. This. Damn. Bag!"

He hammers upon the man's shoulders and head until I suddenly fall forward, free of his weight. A splash in the distance. Joe flops down on the seat next to me, his chest quickly rising and falling. He looks at me and shakes his head. Such a display of quick aggression. I rub the back of my neck. In the distance behind us floats a black-suited buoy of a man.

"They're going to get a boat and come after us. Can this thing out-run them?" I ask the Sailor, who is busy manning the wheel.

"As long as we get around Block Island in time," he assures.

"What's the final destination?" I ask.

"Right now is the best time for me to explain what led to the death of Harold Gordon," the Sailor says. "I don't want you to just know where we are going, I want you know why we're going there. Okay?"

I nod in agreement. It hurts my neck a bit to do so. The discomfort causes me to be reminded of the discomfort in my ear. That is until my attention is diverted to the Sailor's first words.

"Initially, I was a roofer. A seventeen-year-old boy with no college prospects."

Joe and I gather closer.

"My neighbor owned a construction company that did jobs all over Long Island. He got me a job for the summer learning the roofing trade under him. This particular summer we were predominantly doing jobs in Montauk. My brother at this time was a Developmental Engineer for the Camp Hero site, also known as Montauk

Air Force Base. We were both born and raised in Mastic Beach and to be out east together for the summer was great. At night, when he would get the time off, we would go out to the bars and stay up all night. All of us."

"Your brother, you and…" I leave a silent space for him to fill in the rest.

"Carl Miller and Tommy Lansky," he concludes.

Who?" I ask.

"The Air Force at Montauk was transitioning into joining the Semi-Automatic Ground Environment system and the construction of the antennae was at the heart of this all. The ground artillery at Camp Hero was becoming outdated as the Battery Dunns were no longer able to reach the heights of the newer planes that the Soviets were building. They could now fly way above the missile range."

"We are aware of that," Joe says.

"So, the radar surveillance became the new and important task of the Montauk Air Force Base at Camp Hero. It could detect objects in the air up to two hundred

199

miles away. Nuclear missiles were the biggest concern. By this time, Carl Miller and Tommy Lansky were both airmen first class. They lived on the base in the barracks. Carl said he was from Brookhaven and Tommy was an Army brat born on Nantucket. Tommy's father served in World War Two and after he served, he held some high-ranking office in the C.I.A."

"What did Harold Gordon do at that time? I mean, what was his rank?" I anxiously ask.

"Harold Gordon was a bartender."

"He wasn't an officer in the Air Force?"

"No, he was a local bartender at our favorite spot, The Mirage. Out of all the bars at the end of Long Island, The Mirage was the main attraction for the officers of the Air Force when they left the base for the night. We'd go there and drink and dance and even I would pretend to be an active member of the Force to get free drinks sometimes."

"How old was he at the time?" I ask.

The Sailor takes the sea breeze in through his nostrils.

"Harold was about twenty-five. He told us he was born and raised in Montauk and after high school he jumped right into bartending around the area. He was pretty well-known to everybody who drank at The Mirage because he worked there at least five nights a week during that summer. Everybody in the Air Force knew him because he was constantly engaging us in conversation and hooking us up with drinks and meals. We always made sure to take care of him at the end of the night with a good tip. I remember Harold always being fascinated with guys like my brother, your father and Tommy. To him, he was a proud Montauker for life and grew up around all the fishermen and naval officers. His parents were supposedly dead and no longer around. I think he looked up to the servicemen and was always excited to hear stories from them about combat or their worldly travels."

The wind rifles into our faces. The Sailor maintains hand positions on the wheel as I stagger to maintain balance on my feet. I lean closer to encourage him to continue.

"Well," he exhales, "it was late in the summer one night when my brother said he had something really important to tell me and asked that I take a walk around the block with him. He was really anxious, he even made me swear on God, my life and my country that I wouldn't tell anyone what he was about to tell me. I promised I would keep quiet and so he went on to tell me that the Air Force Base had recently been visited by C.I.A. officials. At first, none of the fellow first airmen knew the reason for the sudden visit but over a couple of days of persistent questioning and gossip, word emerged. 'Classified documents regarding the S.A.G.E. radar system had gone missing' he told me. He said that his senior airman overheard his staff sergeant talking about it and then told my brother what he heard in complete confidence. The classified documents were found days later but not where they first went missing and there became a growing suspicion that a mole was present inside the Montauk Air Force Base. They suspected it to be a Soviet who was looking for information on the specifics of the antennae and how it worked.

The senior airman told my brother to keep his mouth shut about the situation and to act as if he had no knowledge of the situation. But, my brother couldn't resist. When he came to me he had such a wide-eyed appearance about himself and he talked with such intensity and excitement. He told me that he was personally going to find out who the traitor was and that when he did they would regret being on the wrong side. I asked him if he had any ideas on who or where to look, you know, if he had noticed anybody acting suspiciously around the base. He admitted that he wasn't the only one who knew about the suspicious activity. Tom Lansky was standing next to him when the senior airman spilled the beans. Afterwards, they both swore to each other to hunt for and find the traitor. Later that night, we met at The Mirage to discuss everything further. Tommy Lansky explained to my brother and me that he had told Carl Miller everything about the prospective 'hunt.'

We gathered together in the corner of the bar, just as we'd done many times before, only this time when we all got together we were all a bit different. We looked strange and... we looked at each other like strangers. Each of us took turns, keeping our conversation low and to ourselves. We recounted the past few weeks and noted anything we'd seen or heard that seemed out of the ordinary. We each took our turns in developing theories and creating suspects. We concluded that it wasn't any one of us but, that it had to be somebody who worked closely with us."

The front of the boat slams down continuously onto each wave the sea offers up in a constant rhythmic pattern that resembles a steady heartbeat.

"Eventually, I remember Tommy looking beyond me, over my shoulder, his eyes seemed to have seen an apparition." The Sailor takes his eyes off the ocean for the first time and looks at me. "It's quite remarkable that I can remember that exact moment, that exact look in his eyes. Memories can be quite persistent whether we want them to be or not."

He turns back to the ocean. "I followed his line of sight over my shoulder and it landed on Harold Gordon. Lansky said, 'what about him?' At first we all sort of brushed it off, citing Harold's likeability and hard-working, high-energetic nature. We all liked the guy, there was nothing not to like about him."

The Sailor pushes the throttle forward and the boat pounds the waves below it, quicker this time.

"But..." He pauses for a moment. "That's all we needed was... a 'but'... a 'what if?'... a 'moment of doubt.' As soon as we could accept the slight notion of Harold possibly being the culprit, we couldn't turn off the stream of possibilities that crossed our minds. We developed fantastical ideas of how and when Harold could've positioned himself into our lives and gotten a glimpse at the antennae papers. I mean, he had visited the base before. He was invited many times because he was close to us all. Not just our little group, but the majority of officers there.

That night, we watched him mingle with everybody at the bar, smile at them, listen to them talk.

We left that night and walked back to the base. By the time we reached the entrance of the base, Harold Gordon was the center of our entire investigation. We all agreed that we wanted proof so, I agreed that I'd monitor him for the week. And that's what I did. For three nights I watched him leave the bar and walk about ten minutes down the road to his house. It was a really small house allegedly left behind by his parents. I'd watch him walk through the front door and less than a minute later the dark home would flicker with one light coming from the same window every time. The window was in the rear, left part of the house and I assumed that's where his bedroom was. I'd hang out for about forty-five minutes to an hour to make sure that he didn't have any visitors or do anything suspicious and he didn't... until the fourth night.

On the fourth night that I followed him home, everything went as usual. He entered the dark house and gave light to the one window in the back. Except this time, about twenty minutes into me hanging around, the front door opened again. I nearly spilled the beer I was drinking. I ducked beneath a tree stump and watched him walk down the driveway and back down the road in the same direction that he came from, back towards town. I followed him until he hit Main Street and made a left. Right there on the corner was the town post office. Harold took an envelope out of his pocket and slipped it through a twelve-inch metal slot built into the front door. Then he walked back to his house.

The next time I saw the fellas I told them what I had seen. Naturally, their suspicions heightened. Carl became visibly upset and wanted to confront Harold as soon as possible. Tommy Lansky had a plan to wait a week and see if this was a routine. So that weekend we played it cool. We went to The Mirage and drank our beers. We interacted with him the way we always had. We listened to him ask us about our week and watched him flash his smile all around the joint. We watched him closely. Then, when they went back to the base at the end of the night, I followed him again. I followed him that night and every night for a week. Even if he didn't work that night, I propped up outside his house and drank a six pack waiting for him to mail another letter. Sure enough, the next Thursday, he did. The same routine: he walked home from the bar, twenty minutes later he came out of his house, walked to the post office and mailed an envelope. I watched this happen for three straight weeks and after three weeks, we had solidified the theory that Harold had copied information from the classified documents and was now mailing that information to someone.

His proposed betrayal became the fury of our conversations. We had such anger at the idea of somebody trying to pull a fast one on us and on our country. We didn't want to confront him face to face until we were absolutely convinced of his treason. So the next Friday, instead of going to the bar we went to his home, when we knew he was working and wouldn't be there.

I took a crow bar to his basement window, went through the house and opened the back door for Carl, Lansky and my brother. I led them straight to the room that always lit up as soon as Harold had entered the house. Sure enough, it was his bedroom. We carefully searched the place. Dresser draws, the closet, clothes. His mattress was turned over, nothing was underneath. There was a desk in the corner that had a bunch of papers and pens on it but when we sifted through the papers there wasn't anything top secret involved, just a bunch of math calculations regarding his bank account. After about thirty minutes, we looked at each other and almost gave up. I swore to them that I had not seen another light turned on in the entire house when he came home every night. I insisted that if there was anything that would prove his guilt it would be in that room. So, we looked at everything one last time. We checked the math on the bank account papers to see if the numbers written down were actually meaningful bits of information about the radar system. Nothing stood out. My brother and I decided we'd check the rest of the house but it only took about fifteen minutes to complete that search. The house was small and its fillings were sparse. The boy lived simply and modestly.

When we returned to the bedroom we found Lansky with a handful of money. A great big stack rolled up. He said it was stuffed inside a hole in the mattress. He counted it and then handed it to Carl. As Carl fingered the money, what was a fairly steady pace started to slow down toward the end. With each green bill that passed through his thumb and forefinger his hands began to move slower and slower. Finally, he stopped completely and began slowly rubbing the dollar bills between his fingers. I caught him inspecting them carefully and asked him what was wrong. He noted that some bills were stiff, almost dried up as if they had been soaked in something. He told me to hold one of the dollar bills as he reached into his pocket and took out a match book. With a quick strike, he lit one of the matches and held it up next to the dollar bill. Low and behold, it appeared right there before our eyes: subtle markings on the dollar bill. Markings that only became visible after heat was applied to the dried-up liquid. At the base, they had all been made aware of the many ways that spies could communicate in cloak and dagger fashion, invisible ink being one of them. Scribbled on this bill, in this type of ink, were facts about the antennae. Specifically, it's coordinates. We looked through the bills and found several more that had been inked with information about the radar system. There were even mentions of McGuire Air Force Base, which was where the data from the antennae was to be sent.

And that was it. The proof that we needed to confirm that Harold had information and he was sending it to someone else. We all became enraged. I remember Carl picking up a lamp off the night stand and heaving it across the room. Harold was so good to us, such a great guy. We felt duped by him. So, we were going to make him pay for it."

The front of the boat slams down onto the ocean.

Boom. Boom. Boom.

The Sailor doesn't look away from the water.

"We waited until he came home from the bar, hiding off to the side of the house. Several times we had to control the urge to meet him right outside the bar because waiting for him was getting everybody incredibly anxious. Again, he went in through the front door and a few minutes later he came out except this time we stopped him right in his driveway. Tommy Lansky was the first to confront him with a dollar bill from his room. Harold denied it and then Carl grabbed the letter out of Harold's hand and tore it open. Inside was money and a letter to his parents. Harold explained that he'd been sending money to his parents in South Carolina every week, but initially Harold had told us his parents were dead so, we all thought this was just a cover and that we had caught him red-handed. We verbally peppered him with questions about who his 'contact' was and demanded that he tell us the truth. We surrounded him, four against one. The confrontation became heavier and more aggressive. I remember it was dark and it was hard to see his face completely, but his voice was a bit shaky. He was becoming more scared as we became more convinced of his guilt. He pleaded with us that we think about what we were saying but we were firm in our beliefs. Stubborn. As the finger pointing continued our anger began to rub off on Harold. He stopped pleading and started to become defiant. He insisted his innocence and even started yelling at us about how offended he was and how he wanted us off his property. He said he was going to call the cops on us for breaking into his house. That's when Carl Miller's right hand came out of the shadows and landed across his jaw. Our friendly ties had officially been fractured. Harold stumbled sideways and began swinging blindly, hitting my brother. So, my brother hit back and Carl followed his first punch with a push and when Harold fell to the ground, Lansky came in with a kick. I joined in and started kicking too. We all started calling him a 'commie' and a 'traitor,' asking him if he thought we were stupid. We were determined to prove a point; we didn't like being betrayed. We didn't have an awareness about us. In that moment, we were riding the wave of pure emotional blindness and attached ourselves to the anger and resentment we were feeling. We were unconscious."

I look at Joe, he's as still as a statue.

The Sailor goes on.

"We continued to beat him up so badly that when we stopped he was barely breathing. All of us exhausted. The deed was nearly done and almost instantaneously we all regretted the extent with which we went after him."

Our boat takes a hard left as we get closer to an island floating up ahead. I've been so taken-in by every word of the Sailor's that, for a moment, I forgot we're not alone. Behind us, in the distance, is a white dot that is our pursuers.

"Now what?" I ask the Sailor.

"Around Block Island, out of their sight line, an old friend is waiting for us with another boat. We're going to switch with him as quickly as possible. Then both of our boats will swing back around the east part of Block Island into view, except, he'll head northeast toward Buzzards Bay and Connecticut and we'll go southeast."

"Towards?" Joe probes.

"Towards Nantucket," he says.

"Because that's where Tommy Lansky lived?" I wonder.

"And because that's where Harold Gordon is buried," he answers.

Chapter 11: Navigating

Around Block Island, out of sight from our pursuers, awaits the other boat. This one's a bit smaller than the boat we're currently riding in and a different color. The Sailor gives a big wave to the man standing on the deck of this new ride. The man smiles, nods and limps to the side of the boat to prepare for us.

The Sailor decelerates and maneuvers our boat in such a way that it slowly pulls up alongside our next ride. The man waits until the boats touch each other and then hooks a rope around to lock the two boats together. He reaches out to take the Sailor's hand and leads him aboard the new vessel.

"Thank you for doing this, Rob," the Sailor says.

"How far back are they?" the man with the limp asks.

"About ten knots or so, we have to move," the Sailor says.

"I understand," Rob takes my hand and doesn't let go until my two feet are steady on board. Joe follows suit. "So, I was thinking of heading into Newport," Rob says.

"The problem with Newport is that it's directly north from here and too close. We need you to be sailing on open water for a bit so that we have a chance to gain separation from you and them," the Sailor explains. "Let us get ahead of you and trail us at about two knots until you see the gap for the Vineyard Sound. Enter in through there and cut through the opening between Nonamesset Island and Woods Hole. That'll take them far enough away from us. When you dock, try to get lost inland before they dock behind you, okay?"

"You got it," Rob nods and looks up at the sky in admiration. "Great day for a ride, huh?"

Joe blows him off with a quick burst of air that exits his nose. "You don't know half of it."

"No," Rob says, his eyes don't come down from the sky, "and I don't need to."

The appreciation in the man's eyes actually makes me look up for a moment myself and notice the sun.

The Sailor moves around the steering wheel. "We're good to go," he remarks.

"Alright well, I wish you fellas the best of luck," Rob smiles and reaches out his hand. I shake it and so does Joe. He hugs the Sailor without a word and pats him on the chest lightly then steps over onto our original boat and unhooks the rope that binds us.

"Thanks again, Rob," the Sailor says and Rob salutes him a friendly manner. He turns his eyes to us and winks. Our boat creeps forward and glances off its counterpart until it completely clears it and gives Rob some room to pull out ahead of us and lead the way around Block Island and back into the wide open Atlantic Ocean. I see no boats behind us.

I make my way to the side of the Sailor and hold on to the dashboard in front of us. "An old friend of yours?" I asks.

"I've known Rob for about twenty years now. He's had his slip at the Marina for as long as I can remember. Longer than me. He's a great fisherman and a great friend."

"That limp, is that an old war wound?" I ask.

"No, well, yes he was in the Navy but Rob's long been a retired real estate agent. The limp is from an accident a few years ago. House explosion. There was a leaking gas pipe in the kitchen and one night the whole place just erupted with him and his family asleep inside. He woke up, leg crushed, fire all around. They pulled him out, but his family didn't make it."

"Then why did he seem so happy, does he drink a lot?" Joe asks.

"No," the Sailor chuckles. "He's not much of a drinker. Rob stays sober for the most part. That's just the way Rob is, he has learned which fire to feed."

"Which fire to feed?" I ask.

"That's right, which fire to feed," he confirms.

"How much are you paying him for this?" Joe asks.

"Nothing," the Sailor replies.

"I don't get it," Joe says. "What's in it for you then? What are you getting out of this? Or is this some sort of guilt-cleansing?"

"No, I forgave myself a long time ago. At first, yes, I experienced it all. All the emotional baggage that comes with the conditioned stories inside the mind. I left here, moved to California, bought a boat, sailed around a bit. Tried to forget about it all but running away never made it actually go away. I ended up coming into contact with a lot of great human beings from all over, which meant I also experienced a lot of different perspectives. One of the biggest experiences and moments for me was when I found myself in the middle of the Pacific Ocean, alone on my boat. I remember, initially, feeling this great big vibration of dread. I couldn't see anything but blue and white all around me for three hundred and sixty degrees and I suddenly became so lonely. I thought to myself, if I died right now I'd have nobody to say goodbye to. Then I noticed the yellow. In the middle of this blinding white and blue was a big yellow ball and it was so warm and so comforting. I let the sun beam upon my skin for what seemed like eternity. I couldn't move. It was as if the whole world wrapped me up in its arms. With my eyes closed, everything seemed to disappear. My skin melted away and the world around me followed thereafter. I forgot I was on a boat. I forgot I was in the middle of the Pacific Ocean. I forgot I was lonely... I forgot it all because at that moment I was feeling such love, such gratitude for my existence amidst this great big world."

Joe rolls his eyes and moves to the back of the boat. Although I could ask the Sailor more about this monumental occasion in his life I can sense Joe's frustration building again, so I turn the discussion around. "How did you find out Harold Gordon was innocent and not a spy?"

"His parents showed up at his funeral."

"But he said his parents were dead," I remember. "So, he really *was* sending them money?"

"Yes. It turned out, a few years back when Harold was a child, Harold's father was involved in a serious car accident. He was drunk and behind the wheel when he drove his car through the front window of a diner, killing a young family. His father went to jail and his mother took Harold down to South Carolina, away from Montauk. Years later, his father was let out of jail and went down to reunite with his family except, Harold didn't want any part of him anymore so, Harold moved back to Montauk by himself. He changed his last name and told anybody that asked that his parents were dead. His mother explained that he was intent on making his own name for himself. I think that's why she laid his last remains on Nantucket, so that he could rest in a neutral place. A place without his family past hovering over him. Sort of a place of his own."

"But why Nantucket, specifically?" I wonder.

"After he laid there on the driveway we knew we couldn't just go to the senior airman and tell him what we'd done. My brother, Carl and Lansky would've been court martialed and I would've been thrown in jail for life

221

no matter what 'right' we thought we had by 'defending our country.' We weren't even supposed to know about the suspicion of espionage so, we tried to cover it up. We went back into his house, cleaned it up, put the money back where we found it, took his surf board and car keys, put him in the back of his own car and drove it down to the beach.

I stole a row boat from the marina, went down the coast and pulled it into the shore of the beach where we parked his car and had his body. We hauled him on board and started to row into the middle of the Atlantic Ocean. We dropped his surf board into the water only about a mile off shore, but we took his body to about the halfway point between Long Island and Nantucket and put him in the water. It was the middle of the night and there was not a light around us. Total darkness. We made it back to Long Island just as the sky began to turn golden with the sunrise.

The surf board washed ashore the next day and because of the parked car on the beach, everyone assumed that he drowned during a midnight surf session.

After a full week of searching, the police declared him officially dead. We all agreed to go to the funeral to keep up with the norm but the whole thing made us ill. I literally vomited several times that day."

"Where was the funeral?" I ask.

"The initial ceremony, with no physical body, was done in Montauk. But it was one year later when fishermen found human bones in their net and brought them back to Nantucket. His mom was convinced they were Harold's and when it was concluded that they were most likely his remains, she decided to have them buried on Nantucket instead of bringing them back to Montauk."

But the money. The supposed silver bullet found in the mattress. The proof.

"If Harold didn't write secret messages on the money then who did?" I ask.

"We've spent the rest of our lives not knowing. We always assumed it was somebody who was in that house when the money was found. Somebody who set him up and then recruited us to help kill him to take the heat off themselves. But, so long as all of us were guilty of the murder, nobody was going to dig any deeper. To save our own ass and keep our own deed in the dark we swept everything to the side and never talked about it again. We never even really spoke to each other much after that. That night destroyed multiple lives and relationships."

"But you think it was… Carl Miller?" I manage to ask. "I heard your brother hint at it before. You think these men chasing us are right about Carl?"

"It seems likely."

Joe's been quiet but I can feel him shifting back and forth like a teapot that's been sitting on the stove for too long. He points to the Sailor. "How do we know it wasn't you? I mean, you killed a man! People go to jail for that."

"Would it make you feel better if I went to jail?" the Sailor solemnly asks.

"Yes! Yes it would," Joe admits, "and if Carl Miller was alive I'd feel better if he went to jail too! But I guess he's paying for it now anyways. It's really hot where he is right now."

Silence on the deck as the boat chugs along. I look to the north; Rob begins to head northeast while we continue due east. South of both of us, a speck chases us along the surface of the water. It's not clear yet if they'll take the bait and follow Rob in our first boat.

"It seems like your father made himself pay for it for the rest of his life," the Sailor notes.

"No, he made everybody else pay for it," Joe raises his forefinger and opens his mouth to talk but nothing comes out for a moment; he's thinking of how to express himself. "I mean, don't you remember?" He turns to me, "Don't you remember how much of an asshole he was to us? To you?" He points his eyes right at me. I could swear it's the most earnest, caring look he's ever given me. It makes me search my memory for the things dad used to do to us and it doesn't take me long to come up with ammunition. My mind always goes back to that one specific moment of mental abuse. It never lays too far below the surface of my being. I can easily recall it at any time. I wonder if Joe is thinking about the same moment. I know he was around when it happened. The look in his eyes tell me that yes, he's on the same wave length as me.

"Remember the shit he did?" he asks.

"Of course I do," I tell him.

"People who are hurt tend to hurt people," the Sailor interjects.

"Shut up," Joe tells him but the Sailor goes on.

"My brother hasn't left this island his entire life. He's chained to it by his pain. He's a selfish, dying, miserable man. Layers upon layers of negativity built up over many years just to try and cover up his pain. Pain that never goes away because he holds onto it so dearly like a safety blanket. You can be mad at your father for his actions, you can want 'justice' for what all of us did. That's fine, that's your prerogative, but can you see that there are so many people who spend their entire lives allowing the wake of the boat steer the ship instead of being their own captains?"

Joe ignores the question. "My father used to tell us how stupid we were." He throws his thumb my way. "Especially him. He used to make him scream it from the mountain tops!" Joe crescendos on the last words of the sentence. "Tell him, Jack! Admit how messed up he was as a father. How he fucked us all up."

The lump in my throat appears instantly as I try to open my mouth. "He did some stuff to us," I manage.

"No," Joe scolds, "tell this man, so that he can stop with his devil's advocate bullshit."

I've always thought about that moment. It has swirled around my head for so many years and I've badly wanted to tell somebody about it. I thought maybe if I could say it out loud it would go away for a while and torture somebody else. But right now I'm hesitant. I'm scared. I feel like I don't want to give a 'poor me' tale. I've gotten this far without telling anybody about it and the weight it holds so, what's a lifetime longer?

"I have no doubt that your father did many things that he regretted," the Sailor starts.

Joe gets fed up and starts to speak the truth. "Carl Michael Miller used to make him stand on a chair and-"

"Back when I was in middle school," the words just spill out of my mouth and cut Joe off. Now that I've started I must keep going. "I remember asking my dad for help with my homework. Now, doing homework with his kids wasn't particularly his favorite pastime to begin with."

"That's for shit sure," Joe interjects.

"I remember us doing some sort of math problems and I wasn't really doing too well with them. I was never good at math. My entire life I just never got it, never felt comfortable with it. And so there we were, doing these equations on this sheet of paper in front of us and I wasn't getting anything right. Every equation he'd ask, 'Okay so, what is the answer to this one?' and I'd look at it and think about it inside my head and then I'd say an answer and I'd see him shake his head and say, 'No. Wrong. How the hell did you come up with that?!' And I'd try to explain myself but of course, because my answer was wrong, my explanation was wrong and he'd let me know it.

I had a lot of math problems that night. Several sheets. It went on like this for a while. We're talking hours," I shake my head as I recall the quantity of my stupidity. "With each equation it just got worse. Sure, I got some right but, not nearly enough. He started yelling at me to write it out on paper and even then I couldn't get the harder ones right. But he could. He seemed to know them all, but it wasn't clicking for me and the more equations we did, the more I got wrong and the angrier he got. And the more intense his anger became, the more afraid I was to even give any answer at all anymore.

Eventually, it wasn't enough for him and he finally snapped and said to me, 'Get up. Get up right now and stand on this chair.' I looked at him completely confused. 'Get up!' he yelled and slammed his fist down and so I slid the chair back and stood up at the table. He pointed at me and said, 'I want you to stand on your chair right now and say as loud as you can- I am a retard.'

I searched his eyes to see if he was serious. He didn't blink. His voice grew with contempt each time he repeated it. 'Stand up on this chair right now and scream as loud as you can- I AM A RE-TARD!'

I shook my head softly. I was in disbelief. The thought of doing it was so humiliating, so frightening. But when I shook my head 'no' at him his jaw squared up and he stood up on his own two feet and towered over me and repeated, 'Stand up. On this chair right now. And scream- I. AM. A. RE-TARD!'

He was relentless. His conviction grew. I asked him why and he told me, 'Because I said so.' As a young boy, what could I do? I can remember tears starting to drip down my face as I put both feet up on the chair. I sort of started hunched over, afraid to stand tall and he caught it right away and told me, 'Straighten your knees and stand up. Own it.' Of course, that only made me feel worse. To be so high up but to feel so small. 'Say it!' he insisted.

I tried to get out of it by telling him how sorry I was. I began intensely apologizing to him. Begging him.

Crying to him not to make me do it. Trying to appeal to him but, he was stubborn in his orders and he didn't miss a beat. 'Say it! Say: I AM A RETARD!'"

I perfectly imitate his voice as I channel that moment with every fiber of my being.

As I tell the story now, out loud and after all these years, the lump in my throat hardens and I have to stop speaking just to force a swallow. If I wanted to cry right now I could, they'd be the tears of my younger self. Decades old yet as fresh as my next breath.

"And so I did," I admit. "I said it, over and over again. A kid, standing on a chair in the middle of the kitchen, screaming his heart out to the man he trusted most."

And then I stop. I don't want to elaborate anymore. I'm embarrassed.

So we sit in silence for a few seconds as the boat rides on.

"I was in my bedroom down the hall and heard the whole thing through the walls," Joe whispers.

I never did get any better at math. In general, I never did as well at school as I should've. I should've been better at a lot of things- academics, baseball, and my occupations. My life should've been better, but that would've required more from me and I didn't have it in me.

"I think if he were here right now," Joe says, "I'd beat the shit out of him, so he'd know what it felt like."

"And what would that do to your anger?" the Sailor asks.

"I don't care," Joe abruptly replies.

"Can you see that your anger is just an emotional layer responding to something else, something deeper?" the Sailor inquires.

"What I see is that I'm the only one who cares about the shit this man did."

"Self-inquiry doesn't imply non-caring," the Sailor says.

Joe turns to me. "Don't you ever get mad about it all?"

"Of course," I tell him and it's true, I do, but not like *he* gets mad. Not physically or verbally like when his face turns red and his arteries raise an inch through his skin.

"Prove it," Joe says. "Show me that you're angry at the man."

"Trust me, Joe, I understand it wasn't fair," I say.

"Fair?! You're damn right it wasn't fair! It wasn't fair to us all those years and it sure as hell wasn't fair to Harold Gordon. This son of a bitch has destroyed multiple lives. In his one lousy, temporary existence he's managed to leave a wake of destruction in his path. Now, I ask you, where is your anger over all of this?"

To explode like Joe does, it reminds me of dad when he does it. I never saw the point of expressing myself in such a manner. My thoughts and feelings were best left inside where nobody else could see or judge. I admit, I do get this little ball in the pit of my chest that feels like one single piece of red coal being fanned by the winds of resentment, but I don't need to acknowledge it on such a grand scale like Joe does. Or like the way dad did.

"Come on. Show me that you're still alive."

"One of the lives your father destroyed was his own," the Sailor speaks.

"I'm talking to my brother," Joe snaps.

The Sailor goes on. "His lack of expressing anger and your propensity to it doesn't make one right and one wrong. It's the lack of understanding it that's unhealthy."

Joe says bluntly, "I don't understand how you can live with yourself."

The Sailor takes a deep breath of sea air in. "Once you do, though, it will be the best day of your life."

I stare at the Sailor. His wrinkles, his hair. His subtle manner. I don't hold the same contempt for him that Joe does. I get it, his past actions are not admirable, but this man I see right now is an old man with a different perspective on things. He seems to know life in a different way and he seems to know more about my father than I do. I don't want to say goodbye to him yet. I want to follow him to Nantucket. I want him to show me more. I want to know more. Am I mad at my father for what the Sailor said they did? Honestly, I'm shocked. The accusations are monumental when I allow them a moment to sink in but, I don't like the way that makes me feel. I reject it all. I don't like the idea of being a product born and raised under such clouds of dark deeds.

I look around us, searching the ocean. It worked. Nobody is following us. No more tail.

If it wasn't Harold Gordon, then who was it? The Sailor and his brother seem to know the answer, but it can't be true. All of this stuff, can it really be true? Maybe I'm wrong about the Sailor. Maybe he isn't a deeper, more experienced man. Maybe he's just nuts. Maybe he's making all of this up. Maybe Harold Gordon isn't buried on Nantucket, maybe there was no such person to begin with.

All I'm certain of right now is that I'm not certain of much. All I can do is dig deeper through all these stories and layers until I find what's at the core of it all and hope that Nantucket holds all the answers.

Chapter 12: Nantucket

I hate the direction in which all of this is heading. *How can we prove that all of this isn't true? There must be a way, an explanation, something...*

With everything that the Sailor has told us, Carl Michael Miller comes out as a murderer and the most probable suspect of international espionage. I'm being directed to believe that this whole trip is one big confession; one big cathartic act of a dying man. I started this search lost, with many questions, and it's safe to say that nothing's changed.

Seeing the shoreline of Nantucket appear in the middle of the Atlantic was a welcoming sight and horrifying reality. Finally, we could get out of this boat but, allegedly, we were soon to be face to face with the resting place of Harold Gordon. Judging by where the sun is, we have a few more hours of light left. The Sailor anchors the boat about twenty yards off the beach. 'Galley Beach,' he says it is. We're fortunate for low tide. We take our shoes off and hold them to our chests as we jump off the side of the boat and walk in knee-deep water until we're on dry land. We put our shoes back on and walk to the parking lot. I have the urn. It is strapped to my back. I don't plan on burying the ashes anywhere on Nantucket, I just don't want to let the urn out of my sight.

The Sailor has already arranged for a taxi to meet us at the beach and take us to Prospect Hill Cemetery.

"Nantucket used to be one of the world's greatest whaling centers," the Sailor tells us as we ride in the cab. "Once the whaling industry declined, Nantucket reinvented itself and became a tourist attraction. Adaptation, flexibility and creativity helped Nantucket survive all these years. The island has created itself time and time again," he says. "I've only been on this island a few times. It took me years before I came to see his grave and usually when I do come to visit I just have a bite and a beer and get back before the sun sets."

I've never been to Nantucket before.

As we drive along, I notice the rich history of the island. In the neighborhoods, some houses are big and new but others are small, older and comforting. Some roads are freshly paved, some are narrow and made of cobblestone and some are just dirt paths. There's family farms and legendary mills and nature preserves.

The entrance gate to the cemetery is a testament to the past. Actually, if there's anything that man can make as a testament to his own memories it's a cemetery.

The taxi pulls in and the Sailor navigates him through the plots.

"I know how to get to the correct plot location, but I don't recall the specific row number," he says. "Stop here." The taxi complies and the Sailor gets out and leads the way.

Joe and I follow him through a sea of stones. Each one representing the parentheses of lives lived in between eternity. There's so many family names etched in a row. It makes me wonder about my family. I guess we'll never be buried together like so many of these people are. My mom's buried in Brooklyn. My dad wants to be buried in Montauk. Who knows where Joe wants to be buried. I, myself, never gave it one thought. Either way, I'm sure we'll be separate in death just like in life.

I get a chance to stare at Joe as I walk behind him. I begin to try and figure out where he and I went wrong. We used to have some really good moments together when we were younger, but eventually he moved out of the house and got married. When I could, I moved into my own place and desperately searched for a steady career to get my parents off my back. As for Joe and I, we started to avoid each other. I can't explain why. If I take into consideration what the Sailor mentioned on the boat then I can start to figure out that our separation from each other, I mean the complete breakdown in communication and the absence of one another in each other's lives, is a result of something deeper. Something that we haven't acknowledged yet. I wish I knew so that I could move past it because I forgot how much I actually enjoyed my brother's company. His attitude and brash, hot-headedness I could do without though, that's for sure. I wish he would bury that part of himself right here in this plot. When he gets like that it makes me start to feel it too and I don't like to feel so... out of control.

"Keep your eyes peeled around here," the Sailor says and we all pay attention to every single headstone as we separate and go down the line, row by row.

"There's some old dates on some of these," Joe notes and I look to concur.

The jingle is heard coming from the side of me. It's the collar of a dog running loose about fifteen yards away. No owner in sight. The dog prances to every other headstone it sees then stops and sniffs and then prances on. He even settles up to one of the gravestones and lifts his leg. *Disrespectful little mutt.* He hears something in the distance: a voice calling. The voice is followed by a figure coming up over the hill about forty yards to our right. The dog runs in the opposite direction of the figure and I watch it disappear amidst the slew of headstones. This approaching person comes into view- it's a woman. She's sweating from her brow and out of breath. She looks miserable and even worse, she's heading right toward me.

"Excuse me!" she yells. I don't look up. I try to ignore her by putting my head down and looking for a headstone that says 'GORDON' on it. "Excuse me!" she yells again and approaches me. "Hello?!" She's too close to ignore now. I look up at her. "Have you seen a dog come this way?" she asks.

"He went that way," I point and start walking in the opposite direction.

"This dog is going to be the death of me," she calls to me. "She never listens, ever. I don't understand it." The woman follows me down a row. "It drives me nuts, I'm two seconds away from having her put down, I swear."

All I can think to do is nod and hum. I don't want to engage her into a conversation. I'm too busy for her problems. I'm pre-occupied with my own at the moment.

"I've tried training her," she goes on, "I'm completely fed up with it."

This lady has to go.

"Honestly, this dog is driving me insane!"

The ringing in my ear starts coming back.

"Do you want a dog? You can have this one." She won't stop. "I'd give it up for one day of peace, that's it."

I nod, but really I want to run away.

Stop talking to me. Go find your dog and leave me alone.

Awkward silence as she huffs and puffs with deep, frustrated breaths.

"Well, I better go catch her," and she stomps away from me.

Thank you.

I wait a few seconds to let her get some distance and when I feel it is safe I look to her. I can tell by the way her hands are moving around that she's talking to herself. She's still cursing that damn dog.

"Found it!" my brother exclaims. His words turn my insides into knots. He and the Sailor huddle up in front of one particular piece of stone. *It can't be real.* I've been hoping, yearning for all of this to be false. A case of mistaken identity or something and the Sailor just being some old man who is terribly confused.

It only takes me a few seconds to meet up with them. I move my eyes down to the name etched in stone and that's when I stop moving all together. *It is real.* Not more than ten feet in front of me is the name that we've been hunting. The name that's haunted my dad for so long: GORDON, HAROLD. BELOVED SON AND FRIEND.

It's official. Everything is actualized.

He is real. And that means so is everything else. His brutal death, the group of young men who are responsible for it and the secret motive that one of them had.

I can feel Joe and the Sailor on each side of me. I reach my two hands toward my armpits and anxiously thumb the straps of the backpack. *I'm still carrying this thing. This thing that I've diligently carried around with me. Before this urn, there was just a note. Dad's note. The spark that put this all in motion.*

Seeing the grave doesn't bring me peace or closure. I'm still lost and now I'm stuck with this hunk of metal inside a bag with the responsibility of disposing of its contents.

This was it? This is what my father wanted us to know? That this man was buried here because of him? Is he looking for some sort of understanding? I mean, he's trying to explain himself, right? That's what all this is about, isn't it? He's trying to tell us that this is why he was the way he was, because of this name, this man and what was done to him. This is my father's confession: that he was a terrible parent because he had done terrible things in the past that he couldn't let go of. Am I supposed to actually feel sympathy for him? Because I don't. I feel disappointed. Disappointed that it's true. I can see that perhaps I'd been blinded a bit about all this and now I think that Joe was right. It was clear cut, black and white: Carl Michael Miller was a bad person, a killer, a spy and anything else you want to label him. It's all fine by me. I don't know how to defend him anymore. I'm not interested in defending him anymore. I thought there would be more. I thought there would be something else but there isn't.

"Are we ready?" Joe asks. "'Cause I've seen enough."

"Let's go," I answer and we back pedal away.

Where do we go from here? I don't know. Honestly, I don't care either. It's over and this is the end of the trail. A dead end. I was hoping that this would conclude differently, but I guess this is my wakeup call and it makes me feel terrible all over. My body constricts in response to my twisted emotions. My hopes are dead, joining everything else in this place.

The taxi drives us to the front gate but slams on the brakes. It's the dog again. He's standing right in front of the entrance. We get out.

"Hey! Get over here," I hear the lady's voice from afar. She runs toward us. "Grab that dog!" she yells.

The dog sees its owner coming and turns on a dime and sprints right into the middle of the road. There's a car heading down the road at that exact moment and it doesn't have much time to react. Tires slide across the concrete as I squint and grimace.

The front bumper of the car stops an inch before the torso of the dog and we all catch our breaths. In response, the dog turns toward the metal predator and begins to viciously bark like a maniac with its nose pointed upward toward the windshield. The driver honks the horn to scare the dog away, but that only makes the dog bark louder.

The owner finally catches up to the scene. "Stop honking!" she yells at the driver. They roll down their window and yell, 'Get your damn dog then!'

"Get over here, what is wrong with you?!" The woman chases the dog around the car with the leash. She tries to grab the dog and when it narrowly escapes capture she stands up and grunts. "What the hell is wrong with you?! Why won't you listen to me?!" In a last ditch effort, she lunges forward and manages to grasp onto the dog's collar and drag the dog away from the middle of the road. The car beeps one last time before speeding.

"Asshole!" the owner yells and then looks down at the dog and groans, "you too!"

Joe is already getting back into the taxi and I quickly follow to avoid any conversation with the woman again as she walks by. *Go home.* I telepathically advise her.

The Sailor walks over to the dog and holds out his hand. The dog licks it before the Sailor pats its head then gets into the front seat.

"We're headed to The Seabed on Main Street, please," he tells the driver.

"Where?" Joe asks.

"This will be the last place I take you," he says.

"And then what?" Joe asks.

"And then the rest of your lives is up to you."

What do I do after all of this is over?

"What's at The Seabed?" Joe wants to know.

"I'm going to show you Tommy Lansky," he says.

"He's still alive?" Joe asks.

"I believe he is," the Sailor replies.

I put the backpack on my lap. I notice Joe glance at it out of the side of his eyes.

"I guess you were right," I say.

"I like hearing that," he tells me, "keep saying it."

"We should just go back to Montauk, put him in the ground somewhere quick and turn ourselves in. Let the police, or whoever, interrogate us and all of dad's belongings. Maybe they'll just give us a slap on the wrist, I don't know."

I'm so dejected, and he can tell. I can feel his sympathetic stare.

"Some parent, huh?" Joe says. "This is why Katie and I don't have any kids."

I'm not sure how to respond to his sudden confession, but it doesn't matter because he doesn't wait for a response before carrying on.

"She wants them; I don't. I say I want to focus on my career and that children cost a lot of money and time but it's really because of one simple thing: I don't want to be a bad father. I don't want to disappoint."

"So, instead, we just get to feel disappointed?" I ask.

"Exactly," he confirms.

"I still don't know what happened to you and me, Joe." I confess to him.

"Don't think on it too much," Joe says.

But it's nagging me. Poking me. Here's a man I really care about and for some reason we drifted apart in such a way that we became complete strangers for a while. *Just like we both did with our father.*

And with that, it begins to unravel. I can't put my finger exactly on what it is so, I begin to focus more. I begin to dig inside of my mind and look at all the inner happenings with great attention.

Just like we both did with our father. I repeat to myself.

We treated each other the same way we treated our dad. And we treated each other the same way he treated us.

In the back of a taxi cab with my brother on my left and my father in a tin can on my lap I get an insight that I have to share. The fruits of self-inquiry.

"Maybe we reminded each other of him and of those moments that weren't so pleasant," I admit.

"I'm sure we did," he adds. "But now, we get to curse his name together," he smiles and looks away. End of conversation.

The taxi pulls over and stops in front of The Seabed Bar and Grill.

"Thank you, sir," the Sailor says.

"Great," Joe claps his hands together, "I can use a drink or ten."

A drink sounds great right now. Something to calm my mind for a bit.

"Do you want me to wait around?" the driver asks.

Joe waves him away.

"We'll be fine, thank you," the Sailor says and hands him some money.

We follow the Sailor into the bar and grill. It's dimly lit. The bar is to the right and three rows of dinner tables are on the left. The Sailor moves straight through the center of the room toward the back wall. As we get closer, the collection of framed photographs hanging on the wall come into clear view. There's probably close to fifty of them, some in color, and some in black and white. The frames on them are either rusted gold or tarnished silver. The Sailor moves through a few of them with his index finger. His brain and appendage work together to mentally scan them all until he stops at one and then turns to me.

"The young man on the right, sitting down on the stool," he notes. "He's holding a pencil and paper in his hands. Does he look familiar to you?"

I look at the Sailor for an explanation but all he does is just twitch his head up toward the framed black and white photo. I step in closer to get a better look. *The young man on the right, with the pencil and paper in his hand. Yes I see him but I don't recog- Oh, I see it now. Yes! Yes he does look familiar!*

"I've seen that face before. His cheek. I've seen that mole on that cheek before," I declare. "That's the doctor!"

"That's Tommy Lansky," the Sailor adds.

Chapter 13: The Writing on the Wall

"Tommy Lansky is the doctor." I make sure I understand that by repeating it to the Sailor.

"When you told me about how this all started you said that you went to deliver flowers to a doctor's office and then everything went haywire after that. I immediately suspected it was Lansky because he's the only one left out of our group who could've possibly known the weight of the name, Harold Gordon. And then you add on the men chasing after you and it made perfect sense. You remember I told you that Lansky was an Army brat and his father held a high office in the C.I.A. I can only conclude that Lansky got spooked and did the same thing my brother did. He called up somebody that he knew, thanks to his father, and reported you and Carl Miller as severe threats to national security."

"But all so quickly?" I ask. "I mean, talk about jumping the gun."

"Don't underestimate the power of fear. As long as none of us talked about Harold Gordon, we felt safe. We thought nobody would ever mention his name again because of the repercussions it might cause for our own well-being and freedom. We wanted nothing more than to forget and ignore that it ever happened and for a long time we did. But threaten to take away a man's freedom and his comfort and I'm surprised they didn't come quicker."

An old man with a white towel slung over his shoulder walks by.

"So, who exactly is Lansky's father?" I ask.

The old man stops behind me. "Lansky?" he asks. "Which Lansky are you asking about?" He looks up at the picture in front of us.

"Tommy Lansky," the Sailor answers. "He's an old friend of mine."

"Uncle Tommy, huh?" the old man's voice cracks and a smile comes to his face.

"Uncle?" I ask.

"Yeah well, not by blood but he used to work for my father in Nantucket's longest-running pharmacy. My father used to love having apprentices working under him, learning the trade. He loved to teach. He taught me everything he knew about pharmaceuticals but the bar and grill business just proved more lucrative in the end. People and beer have better chemistry. Not that I didn't keep the family store running for a long time, but I had to do something else after the fire almost wiped it out completely."

"Is that where this picture was taken? In your father's store?" I ask.

"You bet. That's the two of them hard at work. Even at such a young age he proved a devoted apprentice and friend too; he taught me how to play football and used to take me fishing all the time. He was around and involved so much that he adopted the title 'uncle.'"

"How'd you know that picture of him was here?" Joe asks the Sailor.

"I've been in here before. Saw it once."

"In here? In my bar?" the old man asks.

"Yes, most recently about two years ago," the Sailor says.

"Ah man, friends of Uncle Tommy, huh? It's been ages since I've heard that name." He takes a moment to be nostalgic and then snaps out of it. "Well, can I get you men something to drink?"

"Yes," Joe answers quickly.

"Well come on over," he beckons and leads us to the bar. "But, don't expect no friendly discounts now," he adds.

We take the closest three chairs in a row and the old man settles himself up in front of us and grabs the cloth off his shoulder. "What will you be having?"

"Vodka and soda for me," Joe responds, "scotch on the rocks for him," he points to me. "And whatever he wants," he points to the Sailor.

"Any light beer is fine," the Sailor says.

"You got it," and the old owner goes to fetch the drinks. I set the backpack down next to me.

"Lansky used to tell us all about Nantucket and how much he loved it," the Sailor says. "He'd take trips back here some weekends when he was still serving at the base."

"Then he moved to Long Island and became a doctor?" I wonder.

"I'm not sure about his timeline. After everything happened, none of us talked much. According to my brother, everything at the fort changed. They didn't hang out as a group anymore and so the day their service was up was the last day they ever saw each other."

The old man returns with three drinks. "Here ya go, fellas," he places each drink accordingly.

"Three shots of Jameson, as well," Joe adds.

"That'll cost ya," the old owner says.

"That's fine," Joe replies.

The man fills four shot glasses to the brim.

Joe takes his shot glass and tries to quickly throw it back but the old man shouts, "Wait a second!" Joe freezes. "Cheers," he says and holds his shot glass up. "To the past," and then we knock glasses and shoot the whiskey.

After the old man catches his breath, he turns to the Sailor. "So, do you have any news on Uncle Tommy? Last time I saw him was in the 1960's. Is he even still alive? God, it's been so long. Getting old sucks." He looks at the Sailor. "Ain't that right?"

"Well, apparently he's got a medical practice on Long Island now," I say.

"No way!" the old man yells. "Tommy Lansky has been on Long Island this whole time and he never came back to visit?!" He tries to brush it off but his eyes pause for a second and that one moment of silent reflection speaks volumes about his disappointment. That's when a young girl about mid-twenties comes over and interrupts the old man's grief.

"Excuse me, do we have any more mixers?" she asks.

"Mixers? For stirring drinks?" he asks.

"Yes, exactly!" she emphatically replies.

"You mean these things right here?" he walks no more than two steps to his right and grabs a cup full of plastic, multi-colored mixers.

"Yes, thank you," she reaches for the cup. He pulls it away.

"Did you even look before you asked me where they were?"

"I did."

"I'm willing to bet that you didn't."

She frowns. "Well, I knew that you would know where they were."

"Do you think at all? Or are you perpetually dumb?" the old man pierces her with serious malice.

"I think," she says weakly.

"Take these and remember where you got them from," he violently shoves the cup into her hands and turns his back on her. She slowly creeps away. "Sorry about that, fellas, that's American youth right there."

"New girl?" Joe asks.

"Dumber than a box of rocks," he tells us. "I don't know where she got her ignorant genes from but it sure as hell wasn't me or my side of the family. I blame my daughter's husband. He's an idiot."

"Wait," I say while trying to figure it out. "So that's your…"

"That young Einstein is my granddaughter," he blurts out. "We had high hopes for her when she was younger, but those hopes are fading fast. Her father's a real loser, no brains, no work ethic. I warned my daughter about him before they got married but she was too stubborn to listen. Or maybe she's the one lacking intelligence too, it's a trifecta! You know what makes it even worse?" The man leans in and whispers, "The girl looks just like her father. Dumb *and* ugly."

Wow. Tell us how you really feel. What a dick.

Awkward silence.

261

Joe changes the subject. "So you own this place, right?"

"Yes, bought it thirty-five years ago. Like I said, the pharmacy wasn't pulling in much anymore and my father had already been in the ground for about five years by then. My mother-in-law was long gone too. Hey! Small world," his eyes light up. "You know who my mother-in-law was? Uncle Tommy's Aunt, Dee."

"No kidding," the Sailor remarks.

"You're right, I'm not kidding. Tommy's mother died when he was born and so his Aunt Dee lived with them and took care of the house while Tommy's dad was away in Washington D.C." The old owner shakes his head. "Man that was a long time ago." He wipes a spot on the bar and then resumes. "Anyway, my mother had gotten sick and passed away the year before my father married Aunt Dee. She worked in the store around the same time as Tommy did and she started spending a lot of time with my father. I guess he was lonely and enjoyed the company. He took her places and supported her talents. My father and Tommy's Aunt Dee got married in the summer of '57, I believe."

"What talents did she have?" I ask.

"Oh, she would paint a lot. All sorts of pictures," he says.

"Pictures of what?" the Sailor asks.

"Landscapes like the ocean, mountains or fields of grass. Boring stuff but I mean she did sell a lot of her work though. I think they were all small time sales but she sold them all over to galleries in other countries so, I guess somebody liked them. I still have some of them, they're relics now, dust collectors. When she died, my father took all of her work and hung it around the store as keepsakes. Then when he passed and the fire happened I just put them all into storage, along with everything else that he saved. And my dad saved *a lot*."

Joe leans over and whispers into my ear. "Please don't ask him anymore questions, this man is boring me to tears."

Lucky for Joe, the conversation is broken up when the front door swings open and a party of about ten or so fifty-something-year-olds march in talking and laughing away. They gather at the end of the bar and wave to the old man talking to us.

"I'll be back, fellas," he says. "I have to help this group because I can't trust anyone else to do anything around here." He walks away to tend to his new guests.

This guy is a miserable prick.

The party group explodes with laughter over something that somebody says.

"What do you think the occasion is?" Joe asks.

"Birthday," I guess.

"Must be something exciting," Joe says and then checks his watch. "Can you sail in the dark, old timer?" he asks.

"We still have a few hours of sunlight," the Sailor assures. "You boys want to leave?"

"Sooner rather than later," Joe says and I agree. Today was a horrible day in my life and I'm done. Done with bar owners who are pricks. Done with ladies and their incompliant dogs. Done with men in black suits acting like aggressive assholes.

There's a sudden eruption of laughter and cheers as the older group at the end of the bar raise their glasses to each other and then swig.

At least somebody is having a good day. You know what? I hate them for having a good day.

The old bar owner comes back to us. "Another round, fellas?"

We look at each other.

"Just one more round of whiskey for each of us and then we'll get going," Joe says.

That's fine by me. The owner nods and refills the four shot glasses. One more time we grab our shooters and pour them down our throats. And that's that. One last shot of whiskey with Joe. Maybe the last one for a while.

I notice Joe reach into his pocket and I stop him with my hand. "This one's on me." He shakes me off and continues, but I insist. "Joe, let me do this."

He backs off. The old man puts a receipt on the bar top and I read the total: $35.

I reach into my pocket to find my wallet and take out a wad of money to count. Holding the dirty, green paper between my fingers I begin to count off: 10 dollars... 20 dollars...30, 31... 32... 33... I'm rifling off the bills like Carl Miller did back in Harold Gordon's bedroom. I stop at 35 dollars and put it all down on the bar. The old man takes the pile and turns away.

"I'll get the tip," Joe says.

"You think he deserves one?" I ask.

"We should leave something," the Sailor says.

"I got it, Joe," I flick a few more bills between my fingers and lay them down on the table before Joe does and when the owner returns I look at him, point to the money and say, "that's for you."

Wait.

That's for you. That money is for you to keep.

I go back to the remaining amount of money in my hand.

The dirty, green paper begins to stick to my fingertips as I slowly count again. Eventually I pinch my fingers together and pull out a 5 dollar bill.

Just like Carl Miller did in Harold Gordon's bedroom. I examine the bill. I hold it up to the light. *That's for you.* I told the old bartender. *That tip, those bills are yours to keep. They don't go in the cash register. At the end of the day, the tips go to the bartender. He keeps them... and takes them home.*

Is that how it was done? Is that how Harold Gordon came into possession of money with classified radar intelligence on it?

I look the Sailor straight in the eyes. "Back in Montauk, when you guys were at The Mirage, everybody contributed to the bill?"

"Yes."

"And the invisible ink on the dollar bills, was that a relatively easy thing to accomplish?"

"If you knew how to do it and you had the supplies. They taught my brother and anyone serving at Montauk how to look out for stuff like that."

"But did they have the supplies to do it?"

"It was my understanding that anyone could use something as simple as lemon Juice and a lighter."

I raise my hand to the bar owner to catch his attention. "Do you have lemon juice?!" I yell.

"You guys taking more shots?" he asks.

"No, I just need lemon juice," I tell him.

"What kind of drinks are you looking to make?"

"No drinks, I just need the lemon juice for one second." I don't have time to explain. I hold out my hand in a demanding way.

He gives me a curious eye while his hand searches underneath the bar and quickly produces a small lemon. "I only have lemons. No lemon juice."

I take a straw and a small squirt is produced as I puncture the lemon. Flattening out the 5 dollar bill I begin to write on the piece of dirty, green paper. Every second or so I go back to dip the straw into the lemon to re-wet the tip like I'm writing with a quill and ink.

"Now," as I finish, "we let this dry, right? Then we hold a flame to it?"

"You alright in the head?" the owner asks.

I ignore his question. "Do you have a match or lighter?"

He reaches into his own pocket and produces a lighter. "Don't lose it."

I blow hot air on the bill to expedite the drying process. "Joe, take the lighter," I say and he does.

I take the two opposite ends of the bill and pick it up, making sure to keep the bill as flat as possible.

"Put the flame underneath but move it around so you don't burn the paper."

Joe flicks the lighter and complies.

"Don't you boys burn anything in here. I don't want it to stink!" the owner scolds.

I intensely focus on the 5 dollar bill as the green and white on the surface of it slowly begins to darken. Spots of brown begin to appear. *It's working.* The dark patches begin to connect together to form lines and the lines begin to create words and soon there's a dark brown message revealed on the seemingly innocent face of Abraham Lincoln:

"The Seabed," Joe reads off of the bill.

"That's the first thing I thought of," I say.

"It works," Joe notes, "but how?"

I pick up the lemon and examine it, thinking of the possibilities.

"The fruit juice is dried up by the heat," the Sailor says. "Just like apple slices when you leave them out for too long. They turn brown."

"What were you some kinda boy scout?" the old owner asks.

"Except," the Sailor begins to speak, but stops to stare at the 5 dollar bill in a strange manner.

"Does it bring back bad memories?" I ask him.

"It's brown," he notes.

"Yes," I confirm.

"It's just that… I remember the writing on the bill in his bedroom. It wasn't brown, it was blue," he says.

"Blue?" I ask.

"Blue," he says.

"So, how do we get it to turn blue?" I ask.

"It couldn't have been fruit juice," he suggests.

"Then what else could be used?" Joe asks.

"Some other sort of compound," the Sailor says. "There are plenty of possibilities."

Some other sort of compound. Some other kind of chemical compound.

"Another chemical that reacts to heat? There's probably hundreds or even thousands. And how many turn blue?" I ask.

"I don't know," Joe admits and shifts in his chair as if he's ready to go. "Are you going to leave a tip or not?" he asks.

What kind of chemical compound did a group of teenagers have access to on a military base?

Unless they didn't get it from the base. *No, not the military base, somewhere else.*

"The pharmacy," I whisper.

"What?" Joe asks as he stands up.

"You said Lansky used to come home some weekends."

"That's right," the Sailor nods.

I point to the old bar owner behind the bar. "The pharmacy had to have plenty of chemical compounds in it, right?"

"Of course," he confirms.

"We need to find out which chemicals turn blue when heated. Do you think that's something Lansky would know about? You think your father could have known that and taught that to him?"

"I mean, my father was a chemist, that sort of stuff was right up his alley. Whether he taught that to Uncle Tommy, I don't know."

"What are you getting at, Jack?" Joe asks.

"Lansky was the first person your father sent you to," the Sailor chimes in.

"And he got all these people after me," I added. "He could have easily lied to them about Carl Miller being the spy. You said he had connections, so, he tells them a lie and they pursue it. Taking the heat off of him."

"Where's the proof?" the Sailor asks.

"We don't have any proof because we don't have a time machine to take us back to the 1950's!" Joe blurts out. "We can't go back to see the array of chemicals the pharmacy was stocked with."

"Nope. Only what's left," the bartender adds.

I stop breathing. "What's left?"

"Yeah all the shit that survived the fire. I told you I put it all away into storage along with my pop's belongings."

"Did supplies like chemicals make it out of the fire?" I ask.

"Sure, not many, but there were a few," he answers.

"And you saved them?" I ask.

"I guess I got the hoarding gene from my father. I really should go through it all and clean that basement out down there. I always say I'm going to but, truth is, I think it'll all just stay down there forever. The one time I moved things around down there was when the fire marshal came in here for an inspection and said it was a fire hazard. So I had to get rid of the piles of old newspapers. Like I said, he kept everything."

"You mean to tell me that all of that stuff is here, in the basement of this place?" I ask.

"That's right," the old man answers.

Chapter 14: The Seabed

We need to get into the basement.

"What's all this about?" the old man asks.

"Down there," I mutter.

"Excuse me?" the old man asks.

"The stuff down there." I know where I need to go, but I don't make much sense trying to get there. *We need to get into the basement.*

"What about the stuff down there?" the man asks.

"We may be interested in taking some of those paintings off your hands," Joe brilliantly suggests.

"For how much?" the greedy old man asks.

"Well that depends on what kind of condition they're in," Joe replies and the old man contemplates for a moment.

"It's dusty down there," he says.

"I'm not afraid of dust," Joe says.

"But on the bright side they haven't been touched or messed with. They should be in mint condition."

Joe doesn't miss a beat. "Great, they've been preserved is what you're saying. Give us two minutes to take a look and see if you have anything we can pay you for."

The man twitches his head to the right and walks around the bar. He shoots a glance back at us to see if we're following him and so we jump to our feet and hurry over. In the corner, past the kitchen grill and the dishwasher, there's an old, wooden door. He creaks it open and flicks the light switch on.

With each step downward I feel the steps give a bit with the weight of my body. The temperature drops significantly and the smell grows. The dust hits my nose in a strong wave. My feet hit the concrete and we follow the man past some of the current inhabitants of this cellar: old chairs, wooden tables, baseball memorabilia, photo albums, and children's toys. The old man stops when we get to the back wall. We look down. He bends and grabs a sheet of white cloth that's covering the objects taking up space on the floor. With a slow, deliberate pull he sends a cloud of dust upwards to reveal a stack of paintings. They're bigger than I expected. I'd say about 24 x 36 with wooden frames. We pick them up and check them out. Landscapes indeed: farmlands, woods, a boat on the ocean and snow- covered mountains. They're not very well painted landscapes though. Definitely not worth my money. The old man, thinking that we're interested in buying one of these from him takes them and props them up on the ground by leaning each one against the wall so that we can see them, displaying six in all.

"Not only are they nice pieces of art but they're vintage now." After the sales pitch, he steps back to look at them all. "What do you think?"

I get a quiet tap on my back from Joe. With a subtle glance and movement of his eyes he draws my attention behind us. There it is: a great big shelving unit. It's about six feet high with about seven shelves full of glass jars, masonry jars, growlers, wooden boxes and more.

"Um..." I stall for a second... "Can we have a minute to think this over and talk amongst ourselves, in private?"

The old man sighs. "I suppose. I gotta go back and check on the bar, anyways. Don't take too long, I don't have all day."

He shuffles back to the wooden steps and climbs out of sight. Joe and I rush to the shelves and begin to search. Bandages, gauze, pill boxes. Joe flicks the lighter and takes the flame to the mason jars, pill boxes and glass containers. Some have pills inside of them, some hold liquids.

"Acetylasalicyclic acid," Joe stumbles as he reads the labels.

I toss boxes around. I rub bottles to try and read the labels. I rummage through a pile of gauge.

"Aluminum Hydroxide," Joe continues, "Dextrose... Cobalt Chloride... Magnesium Carbonate." The flame extinguishes. "Most of these bottles don't even have labels anymore. Do we even know which one we're looking for?" He snaps the lighter on again. I look at the Sailor for the answer to that question.

"I'm not sure of the exact names of the chemicals," he says.

"So we don't even know what we're looking for?" Joe admits. "Great."

I close my eyes and exhale with sheer disappointment. How stupid could I be? We don't even know what we're looking for. We're blindly trying to prove a hunch. A hunch we don't even know how to prove! I don't know anything anymore. I thought we had something, but there's no proof. There's nothing but the remnants of other people's lives down here. I got so excited, over what? A brief flicker of hope? *Hope is dead.* My ear starts throbbing again.

That red coal in the pit of my stomach begins to heat up. This acknowledgment of defeat fans the coal. These feelings of failure and embarrassment fan the coal. It gleams brighter, redder. I grab a glass bottle off the shelf. My father being a murderer fans the coal. My father being a liar and a traitor fans the coal. Me being his son fans the coal until a tiny flame ignites on its surface. I grip the glass bottle tighter. Images of Harold Gordon's grave fan the flame. That fucking lady and her fucking dog fan the flame. Being chased around Long Island fans the flame. It flickers into a fully-fledged fire. My useless, uneventful life fuels the fire. My failed life fuels the fire. Standing on the chair as a young, innocent boy, fuels the fire until the glass bottle I'm squeezing begins to burn my hand the way the pit of my chest burns with anger, hatred and resentment. I can't take it anymore. I can't stand the fire anymore. I can't hide the pain anymore. My chest erupts, my hand explodes and I heave the bottle across the room with such rage and such power. The glass shatters against the back wall and the chemical content splashes all over.

It feels so good. I grab another glass bottle.

"Fuck you!" I scream and heave the bottle across the room again. "I hate you!" And I grab another glass bottle and another and another. They crash against the wall and spray chemical liquid all over.

"I can't take it anymore! I hate you so much! You're lucky you're dead, because if you were here right now I'd smash your head against that brick wall myself!" I'm unconscious. Like a nuclear warhead on autopilot. My words flow out from the fiery depth of my heart into the cold, dark, dusty air of the basement. When I run out of glass bottles on the shelf I still go on to hurl words of truth out towards the image of a man who's no longer here in person but very much alive in the hidden corners of my mind.

"This whole time," I shake my fist, Joe stares at me with wide-eyed anticipation. "This whole damn time I tried to give you the benefit of the doubt. This whole damn time I tried to find one fucking good thing that you've done. Something to hold onto. One thing to cling to so that I could call you my own. So that I could feel some shred of validation for attaching myself to you for all these years! So that I could justify ever allowing you into my mind and soul and giving a shit about what you thought of me and my accomplishments or lack thereof. How I ever thought that you could've had an ounce of decency in you is beyond me. You're nothing special.

You're no hero and you're no martyr. You're no murderer or traitor to me either. You're dead, plain and simple. You're nothing except a ghost, terrorizing me still, to this day."

I stop after my last words.

That's it.

He's always been terrorizing me, back then and still now.

I am a retard.

I can hear the tone of my own voice at the tender young age at which I was forced to say those words. That boy who uttered those words over and over once had faith. Faith in the people around him. Faith in himself.

"You fooled me," I whisper and try to catch my breath. "You betrayed my worth."

I pick my chin up and Joe is no more than an inch away. He squeezes the hell out of me. I bury my face into his chest. "I wanted so badly for him to be something else."

Joe rubs my back and then grabs my shoulders on each side and pries me off of him in order to look me in the face and say, "I'm proud of you," and then he hugs me again. My chin wraps around his shoulder and I crunch my eyelids together. When they open, my sight falls on to the carnage of shattered glass bottles. Chemical liquids of all kinds drip down the wall and onto the paintings that are on display below. The basement door swings open and hurried footsteps follow. He must've heard the commotion. He's going to be so pissed.

"What the hell is going on down here?!" the old owner exclaims from behind me.

I feel Joe begin to loosen his grip on me. I'd turn around to face the man but I can't; the color catches my attention. My eyes won't move. The color starts faint but with each drop of chemical liquid that spills over the frame and onto the canvas the color brightens until it's clear. Clear, bright and blue.

"I said, what the hell is going on down here?" the man repeats.

Joe steps back to look at me. "You're okay, Jack," he says in a soft, comforting tone, but I can't give him any acknowledgement that I hear him. The blue color on the paintings begins to twist and curve into patterns and the patterns become shapes and the shapes become pictures and words. Joe spins to see it for himself.

"No. Fucking. Way," he remarks and we rush over to inspect. All six paintings have some remnants of blue being revealed beneath the array of colors that were brushed onto the canvas. Whatever chemical that I threw against the wall is now mixing into the invisible ink that was etched into the paintings.

"What the hell did you guys do?! You've ruined them!" the man yells.

"No," the Sailor counters, "he revealed them. Look at this one." He points to one landscape painting that seems to have gotten the wettest. I can make out a blue diagram drawn into it. "This is a drawing of the antennae, with the parts labeled," the Sailor says.

We huddle around it.

"What the hell is going on?" the man says.

"Do not touch these paintings," the Sailor demands.

"His aunt?" I wonder aloud.

"Lansky was feeding her information and she was 'selling' it overseas," the Sailor notes.

"Back to the homeland," I add.

"Unbelievable," Joe concludes.

"This is our proof," I say. "We need to call the police. Forget running from the men in black suits, once they see this we're no longer necessary to them."

Joe puts his arm around me. I reciprocate the gesture and pat him on the back and shake my head in amazement. Then I walk past everyone and shuffle across the floor and up the stairs.

Damn. That's all I can think. *Damn.*

I rise from the basement and work my way through the kitchen and passed the bar top. A woman laughing uncontrollably bumps into me.

"I'm sorry," she says, then she examines me. "Care to celebrate with us? You look like you could use a drink."

I look her up and down myself and scan her group of friends partying behind her. All of them hold cocktails and wear smiles. "No… What's the celebration, anyway?" I ask.

"My sister's funeral," she replies.

"You're celebrating your sister's death?" I ask with disdain.

"No, of course not, we're celebrating her life!" the woman shouts and they all cheers behind her and take a sip. "It wasn't always pretty but, damn it was beautiful. It was an incredible piece of art she called her life."

That strikes me. Hits me, actually.

Like a kick to the chest. I'm speechless, breathless.

And like that, I walk away, step outside into the light and feel complete clarity.

Which fire am I feeding?

The question hits me like the sun hits my skin and the answer lies intertwined within the warmth. I walk about twenty yards down the sidewalk until I reach the Nantucket Basin where plenty of boats are docked. I plop down onto one of the benches that over-look the water. The thoughts inside my head thrash around but I don't try to understand them all. I don't judge them. I am more or less just allowing all of them to unfold before my mind's eye.

I have a choice.

Was it always like this? Have I always been blind to see the space in between all situations? I feel like I've been aware of it but never believed in the totality of its power.

Why? Because I allowed the power to be taken away from myself. I allowed someone else to tell me my worth all those years ago.

I stay in this mode. I keep peeling back the layers:

Dad never found the power in the space in between all situations and so he trained me to be just as ignorant. He passed it down and I accepted it.

Holy shit.

It's not him I've been so angry with for so long. It's myself. It's always been myself. I *allowed* him to betray me. Yes, I was young and didn't know better but now, I have no excuse. I can see now; that poor boy who gave away his power and self-worth never healed. He still hates himself for allowing himself to get hurt.

I notice Joe and the Sailor approaching. They sit down on the bench beside me. The three of us look out onto the water.

"I never forgave my father, because I never forgave myself," I acknowledge.

"It's not your fault," Joe says.

"You're absolutely right," I confirm. "I was terribly confused. So many people and so many events all in the end either feed the fires of love and choice or the fires of fear and confusion. It depends on which you decide on." Never before have I spoken like this. Never before have I enjoyed such an incredibly different perspective.

The Sailor speaks. "That's what I realized that day in the middle of the Pacific Ocean as the sun engulfed my body. I realized, that I could either feed the fire of my worried, scared, small mind. Or I could embrace the ever-present, gigantic world of experience."

"I don't want to forgive him," Joe admits. "I don't want to give him the satisfaction."

"Forgiveness is never about the other person. It's about allowing yourself to feel good. It's an act of self-love," the Sailor says. "Your life is your life. May it be a masterpiece of experience and nothing else. Forgiveness allows experience to continue to flow. It allows life to flow and allows you to enjoy it… all of it."

Joe doesn't tell him to shut up. He doesn't have a comeback this time.

We sit there for a few moments and allow the world to be as it is. Tiny waves crash on the shore of the boat basin but the water never stays, it always retreats back into the larger body where it creates another new and different wave. Where I go from here is up to me. I begin to ponder the possibilities of my future but I'm reminded of one tiny task that I still have left. A task that I feel in my heart I must do. I must bury my father in Montauk where his younger self died all those years ago.

"The urn," I remember. "I left it at the bar."

"Don't worry about that thing, man. It's over. Done with. We called the cops, everybody will be here soon. We can go home. Finally." Joe says.

"No, it's okay. I'm okay. I'm going to bury him, once and for all. Not out of spite or haste, but for closure."

"Where?" Joe asks.

I can only think of one place. I lean forward to see the Sailor. "Take me to where Harold Gordon used to live."

The Sailor nods.

Chapter 15

Today will not be the last time I see my brother. I promise myself that.

He insisted on staying on Nantucket and explaining to the authorities everything about the paintings and our newfound evidence. I practically begged him to come with me to bury dad, but he wouldn't budge. Eventually, I had to understand. This incredible idea of forgiveness for the sake of one's own health is a new revelation that will take time and commitment. So, I didn't keep pushing it on Joe to come. Instead, I allowed him to be where he was with himself; where he is in his life right now.

The Sailor and I remain relatively quiet the entire boat ride back to Montauk. The sight of the east end of Long Island as the sun sets is a great moment for the both of us. It's warm, quiet, and soothing. I was in such a rush to drive out to Montauk in the first place that I never took a moment to take in its incredible existence.

"What was it that you said the first time we met you?" I ask him.

The Sailor recites, "All this time and the sun never says to the sky, 'You owe me.' Look at what happens with a love like that."

Damn right.

Our taxi arrives at an empty lot of brush, weeds and trees. No house. Just unkempt growth.

"This is it?" I ask the Sailor.

"Yes."

"Why did they knock down his house?" I ask.

"It became such an eyesore after years of being empty and falling apart."

"When did they knock it down?"

"Years ago."

I walk to the middle of the lot, the Sailor waits by the taxi and lets me go alone. Just me and the backpack. *What a relief,* I think, as I pull the straps off my back for the last time.

I bend down and find a good rock to start digging with.

What a ride. Not just the last few days but, everything. What an incredible trip. A week ago I had no idea of the things that were going to transpire. The spectrum of emotions and thoughts that I've experienced can't be taken away from my story line. Because of all of this and everything that I've experienced, I am fuller. What an incredible gift to be human.

The hole is finished. I drop the rock and take the urn out. It's still got a shine about it. Decades of mortal wear and tear placed inside a brand new, shiny tin. As I unscrew the lid I can feel closure. My father wanted to tell me something and I listened. He said, "I hope you will do the one thing I couldn't do." I've done that too and I will continue to do it every day.

"Thank you," I say as I unscrew the lid and grab the bottom of the urn and begin to turn it upside down. I hear a scraping sound trickle down the inside of the urn. I've never seen human remains in ash form before and it appears that I'll have to wait another day to do so because the contents inside the urn aren't ashes; just a note. I shake it for more. Nothing. I look at the urn as if maybe I've picked up the wrong one along the way. Nope, no mistake.

I unfold the piece of paper:

"If you're reading this then I hope you've been successful. If you've completed the trip to Nantucket then I hope you know the truth about what we've done and also, who Tommy Lansky really is. The authorities will look for him at home and at his office, but I'm sure he will not be there. Lansky is a dangerous man right now. He knows a lot of secrets. Think of how much intelligence he and his family have accumulated after all their years of 'service' to the U.S. government. The work he did in Montauk is only the tip of the iceberg. Lansky is involved in a serious government conspiracy that permeates through to the top of the chain. His capture now would be a threat to those who play a role in this conspiracy. It's simple, he knows too much to be caught alive. So, Lansky will try very hard not to be captured by the authorities while at the same time he will try not to be killed by his

conspirators. This means that he will never see us coming. Help me find Tommy Lansky, alive, so we can properly expose him once and for all. I have a good idea about where he is headed so, leave the urn, pack a bag, and find me on Fire Island."

I need a moment to process this information before responding...

Son of a bitch.

90478417R00177

Made in the USA
Middletown, DE
24 September 2018